D0126743

THE FUR HAT

BOOKS BY VLADIMIR VOINOVICH

The Life and Extraordinary Adventures of Private Ivan Chonkin

The Ivankiad

In Plain Russian

Pretender to the Throne

The Anti-Soviet Soviet Union

Moscow 2042

THE FUR HAT

VLADIMIR VOINOVICH

Translated from the Russian
by Susan Brownsberger

HARCOURT BRACE JOVANOVICH, PUBLISHERS
SAN DIEGO NEW YORK LONDON

HBJ

Copyright © 1989 by Vladimir Voinovich
English translation copyright © 1989 by Susan Brownsberger

All rights reserved. No part of this publication may be reproduced or transmitted in any form or by any means, electronic or mechanical, including photocopy, recording, or any information storage and retrieval system, without permission in writing from the publisher.

Requests for permission to make copies of any part of the work should be mailed to: Copyrights and Permissions Department,
Harcourt Brace Jovanovich, Publishers,
Orlando, Florida 32887.

Library of Congress Cataloging-in-Publication Data
Voinovich, Vladimir, 1932–
The fur hat.
I. Title.
PG3489.4.I53H38 1989 891.73'44 88-26803
ISBN 0-15-139100-9

Printed in the United States of America

First edition

A B C D E

THE FUR HAT

Whenever Yefim Semyonovich Rakhlin was asked what his next book would be about, he lowered his eyes, smiled, and replied, "I always write about decent people."

And his whole manner suggested that he wrote about decent people because he himself was decent and saw only the good in life, that the bad did not exist for him.

His heroes were members of the "fearless" professions—geologists, mountain climbers, cave explorers, volcanologists, polar research workers—men who struggle against the elements, that is, against a force free of ideology. This allowed Yefim to tell stories in which regional, district, and Party committees were little involved (a point of great pride with him), and at the same time to get his books out as fast as he wrote them (approximately one book per year), without any trouble with the censor or editors. Many books went on to become plays, film scripts, and radio and television shows. This had a very positive effect on the author's standard of living.

His five-room apartment was packed with imports: the living-room set was Rumanian, the bed Arabian, the upright piano Czechoslovakian, the television Japanese, and the refrigerator was from Finland. He decorated the apartment with objects brought back from his many expeditions. Hung on walls, spread on the floor, arranged on windowsills, bookshelves, or special stands were antlers, a walrus tusk, a stuffed penguin, a polar-bear skin, a giant tortoise shell, dried starfishes and sea urchins, skeletons of deep-sea fish, Nanay moccasins, and Buryat and Mongolian clay figurines. As he showed the collection to visitors, Yefim would say reverently, "This was a gift from the petroleum workers. This, from the cartographers. This, from the speleologists."

In the press, Yefim's works were usually received favorably. True, it wasn't the literary critics who reviewed them, as a rule, but those same spelunks (as his friend Kostya Baranov called all fearless people, regardless of their profession). The reviews—I suspect Yefim wrote them himself—were all similar and had titles like "A Needed Book," "Useful Reading," or "A Fact Everyone Should Know." They said that the author knew the life of his heroes well and that he described the romance of their dangerous and difficult work authentically.

Yefim assured me that his characters—upright, handsome, one better than the next—were true to life. I was skeptical.

In my opinion, people everywhere are alike: even on an iceberg, a Soviet collective will have its careerists and its stool pigeons, and at least one KGB agent. And then, under conditions of isolation and prolonged separation from their homeland, even people of great courage may finally weaken and exchange jokes of dubious political content. And if their iceberg drifts to some Western shore, they might not all return.

When I expressed this thought to Yefim, he told me hotly that I was wrong: under extreme conditions, decent people rose to the challenge.

"What challenge?" I asked. "The challenge of returning or the challenge of not returning?"

In the end, Yefim would stop talking and purse his lips. There was no point arguing with me: in order to understand high ideals, one must have them oneself.

In Yefim's novels you invariably had a fire, blizzard, earthquake, or flood—with such medical consequences as burns, frostbitten limbs, and drowning victims in need of resuscitation. The decent people would run, fly, swim, or crawl for help, would unhesitatingly share their blood, skin, extra kidneys, and bone marrow, or display their fearlessness in some other admirable way.

Yefim himself was fearless. He could tumble off a Pamir cliff, nearly drown in a polynya, or get burned fighting a fire at an oil well. At that same time he dreaded the number thirteen, black cats, viruses, snakes, dogs—and tyrants. Everyone he had to ask a favor of was a tyrant. Tyrants, therefore, included magazine editors, the secretaries of the Writers' Union, policemen, janitors, ticket sellers, store clerks, and apartment-house managers.

Whether Yefim approached those tyrants with large or small requests, he would put on such a pitiful face that only the stoniest heart could refuse him. He was always groveling. He groveled for important things, like the reissuing of a book, and for the most unimportant, like a subscription to the magazine *Science and Life*. His campaign to have the *Literary Gazette* observe his fiftieth birthday with an announcement, a photograph, and some sort of medal—one could write an entire short story about that. Even a novella. Yefim was only partly victorious in that battle. The announcement appeared without a photograph, and instead of a medal he got only a certificate of distinction from the Central Trade Union Council.

Yefim did have some metal decorations. Toward the end of the war, by adding a couple of years to his age in his documents (he was fearless even then), he got into the army, although he never made it to the front—his troop train was bombed and he was wounded. For his failure to participate in the war he was given the Victory Over Germany medal. Twenty years and then thirty years later he received anniversary medals for the same thing. In 1970 he got a medal in honor of Lenin's centennial, and in 1971, the Opening Up the Oil and Gas Deposits of Western Siberia medal. This medal was pinned on Yefim by the minister of oil and gas in exchange for a copy of his novel *Oiler,* which had been dedicated, however, to the oil workers of Baku and not of western Siberia. The above-mentioned medals added shine to Yefim's résumé and permitted him to remark modestly in biographical blurbs, "Have been decorated by the government." Sometimes instead of "government" he wrote "the army." It sounded better.

Yefim usually visited me on Thursdays, when he went to the store across from my house to be issued, as a war veteran, Polish chicken, fish sticks, a package of buckwheat, a jar of instant coffee, and a box of those stuck-together candied lemon wedges. He carried all this in a large attaché case that held other groceries bought along the way, in addition to a couple of copies of his most recently published novel—gifts in case he met any useful people. The same attaché case also contained a new manuscript, which he always showed his friends, among whose number I was included. I'll never forget that thick yellow folder with brown strings and the inscription "File No."

Setting the attaché case on a chair, Yefim would carefully extract the folder and hand it to me as if embarrassed yet with the air of according a rare honor. Not everyone was so honored (and many, truth to tell, were all too glad not to be).

"You know how important your opinion is to me," he would say, averting his eyes.

Sometimes I tried to get out of it. "Why do you want my opinion? You know I quit criticism. They won't let a person do it seriously, and if you can't do it seriously, it's not worth doing. I work at the institute, I get a salary. I'm not about to start reviewing books. Not yours, not anyone's."

Then, blushing, he would assure me that he wasn't asking for an actual review—just my highly authoritative verbal opinion. And of course I always gave in.

One day, though, I blew up and said, not to Yefim but to my wife, "I'm going to tell him, this time, that I haven't read his book, that I don't intend to read his book, that I've had it up to here reading about decent people. Give me villains, give me losers, scum, Chichikov, Akaky Akakievich, Raskolnikov! A man who kills old ladies! A deserter who sells stolen dogs!"

"Now, don't get excited," my wife said soothingly.

"Look at the first few pages, at least. You never know, there may be something there."

"I don't even want to look. There can't be anything there. A crow doesn't suddenly start singing like a nightingale."

"At least flip through it."

"There's no point even in doing that!" And I hurled the manuscript across the room. The pages went flying.

My wife walked out. After I cooled off a bit, I began to pick up the pages, glancing at them and waxing indignant over every line. I ended up flipping through the manuscript, reading several pages at the beginning, and glancing at the middle and the end.

The novel was called *Ore!* One of the members of a geological expedition breaks his leg. At first he fearlessly tries to conceal this fact. The nearest doctor is a hundred and fifty kilometers away, and unfortunately the expedition's all-terrain vehicle has broken down. So the decent people decide to carry their comrade through rain and snow, through marsh and mud, in the face of incredible difficulties. The patient, though fearless, is not too bright. He asks his friends to leave him at the site, since they have discovered a vein of ore that the state badly needs. And if the state badly needs it, it is more precious to him than his own life. (For decent people, something is always more precious than their own lives.) The hero is naturally rebuked by his decent comrades. They will not think of abandoning him in his misfortune. The supplies are gone, no food, no tobacco, and the temperature falls below zero, but they carry their comrade all the way. They do not abandon him, they do not shoot him, they do not eat him.

It was clear. I jotted down a few notes on a sheet of paper and waited for Yefim. I would tell him the truth.

He came on Thursday as always, burdened with his stuffed attaché case. From it I was given a jar of poor man's (Bulgarian) caviar.

We talked about this and that, the latest Voice of America broadcast, our families, his son Tishka in graduate school, his daughter Natasha living in Israel. We discussed a certain very bold article in the *Literary Gazette* and weighed the chances of the Conservatives and Labourites in the upcoming elections in England. For some reason the Conservatives and Labourites in England always excited Yefim; he would repeat to me what Neil Kinnock had said to Margaret Thatcher and what Margaret Thatcher had replied to Neil Kinnock.

There was no avoiding it any longer. I told him, finally, that I had read the manuscript.

"Oh, very good!" With anxious haste he drew from his attaché case a medium-sized notepad with Yury Dolgoruky on the cover and from his pocket a Parker pen (gift of the oceanologists). Then he looked at me expectantly.

I coughed. I could not begin right off with a devastating blow. Better to sweeten the medicine first by saying something positive.

"I liked . . ." I began, and Yefim, the pad supported on his knee, scribbled rapidly, diligently, leaving out not a word.

"But what I didn't like . . ."

The Parker pen lifted from the pad. A look of boredom appeared on Yefim's face. He was looking at me, but he wasn't listening.

This was not deliberate; Yefim had the kind of mind that takes in only what is pleasing.

"You're not listening," I said.

"No, no! Why?" Flustered, he brought the pen back to the paper, poised to write, but still not writing.

"It seems to me," I went on, "that when a man breaks his leg, no matter how fearless and decent he is, he thinks about the leg—at first, at any rate—and not about the fact that the state needs ore of some kind."

"Cobalt ore," Yefim corrected me. "The government needs cobalt badly."

"Yes, I understand. Cobalt ore—of course we need it. But if it's been lying there millions of years, surely it can lie there a few more days. It isn't going anywhere. In the meantime, his leg . . ."

Yefim shook his head. He pitied me, a stranger to noble impulses, but he knew that it was fruitless to argue. If a man lacked something, he lacked it. So Yefim, continuing our discussion on a lower plane, asked what I thought of the overall structure of the novel, and of the *writing*.

The writing, as always, was abominable. But I saw in his eyes such a desperate desire to hear praise that my heart quailed.

"Well, the writing is . . ." I cleared my throat. "It's . . . all right." I looked at him and changed that. "It's not bad, it's . . . actually rather good."

He beamed.

"Yes, I think that the style . . ."

For such writing a man should be shot. But, with

Yefim looking at me, I mumbled that as far as style went, he was in good shape, though there were a few rough spots—

Here he reached into his pocket for a handkerchief or a Valadol, and I realized that even a few rough spots might be enough to bring on a heart attack.

"*Little* rough spots," I hastened to add. "Anyway, that's only my opinion, my subjective opinion, they've always criticized me for subjectivism, you know. But *ob*jectively, on the whole, this is good. Even terrific."

"How did you like the part where Yegorov, on his back, looks up at the Big Dipper?"

Yegorov was the hero. I couldn't recall anything having to do with the Big Dipper, but I said that I had loved it.

"And the scene at headquarters, in the chief's office?" Yefim was spurring me to a higher pitch of enthusiasm.

Good God! What chief? I had thought that the action all took place outdoors, in the wild.

"Ah, yes, yes," I said. "At headquarters. That was wonderful. And the title, don't you think, is very appropriate," I added, to get away from these details.

"Yes," Yefim said, warming up. "Yes, I wanted something that would express the higher idea of the book. Because it's not just the ore in the earth, it's the ore in each of us. . . . Remember when they bring him to the hospital? And they see that silhouette in the frozen window?"

I didn't remember that either, but I nodded approvingly. To avoid any further questions, I jumped up and congratulated Yefim on his success. Though I couldn't look him in the eye.

My wife fled to the kitchen, and I heard her out there choking with laughter. But Yefim rushed over and shook my hand.

"I'm glad you liked it," he said excitedly.

After leaving me, he promptly spread the news of my praise all over Moscow. I got a phone call from Baranov. Lisping more than usual, Kostya wanted to know whether I really liked the novel.

"What's the problem?" I asked, on my guard.

"The problem," Kostya said angrily, "is that you are fortifying Yefim in the absurd idea that he's a writer."

For, you see, though Kostya was Yefim's closest friend, he never spared him. He considered it his duty to tell him the truth, no matter how unpleasant. I was surprised that Yefim stood it.

Yefim lived on the sixth floor of the writers' building near the airport metro station—a convenient stop. A clinic downstairs, the Literary Fund's cooperative across the way (a minute's walk), the metro to the left (two minutes), the Komsomol grocery to the right (three minutes), and just a little farther—within walking distance, as the Americans say—were the Baku Cinema, the Leningrad Road Farmers' Market, and the Twelfth Precinct police station.

His apartment was large, and it became even larger when his family was reduced by one-fourth, which occurred when his daughter left for her historic homeland, namely, Tel Aviv. Natasha's departure caused fireworks.

To understand the reason for the fireworks you have to know that Yefim's wife was an ethnic Russian—Zina Kukushkina, from Taganrog. Kukusha, as Yefim affectionately called her, was a round, bosomy, lusty, empty-headed lady with big ambitions. She smoked long foreign cigarettes that she got through her connections ("on the side," as they say), drank vodka, sang bawdy songs, and swore like a trooper. She worked as a senior editor in television, the Patriotic Education Department, and produced the program "No One and Nothing Is Forgotten." She was also secretary of the Party organization at the studio, a deputy to the District Soviet, and a member of the Science Society. But under her bra she wore a cross, and believed in mummification, telepathy, and the laying on of hands. In brief, she was a fully modern representative of our intellectual elite.

Kukusha had kept her maiden name to avoid blighting her career, and for the same reason had made both her children Kukushkins and registered them as Russians. Her strategy proved correct. She got ahead in her own career and did what she could to further her husband's literary progress.

Though well over forty now, she still had lovers. Military men, usually. Of these the most important was General Pobratimov, twice a Hero of the Soviet Union. He and Kukusha had become acquainted long ago, when he was still deputy minister of defense. The general recognized her on television. He was so smitten that he undertook to serve as consultant for the broadcast of "No One and Nothing Is Forgotten." I am told that sometimes, when Yefim set out with fearless people on distant missions (or, as Kostya put it, in search of dumbass adventures), Pobratimov would send a long black car with his aide, a short, potbellied colonel named Ivan Fedoseevich, to fetch Kukusha. And this would happen during the day, during working hours. Ivan Fedoseevich would enter the editorial office in a uniform bedecked with ribbons, greet all Kukusha's colleagues in a highly unmilitary manner, show all his gold teeth in a broad smile, and announce with a leer, "Zinaida Ivanova, you are expected at General Headquarters with the materials."

Kukusha would throw some papers into a folder and leave. What people said behind her back did not greatly concern her.

When the general himself visited Kukusha, a traffic policeman would first appear in front of her building. Then some men who looked like plumbers would arrive in two Volgas and station themselves around the premises. On these occasions, no matter what the weather, a couple, a pair of lovers, would sit on the bench at the entrance. While they drank wine from a bottle or embraced, the man would open the woman's blouse (so Kostya described the procedure to me) and murmur into her bosom, which probably cradled a hidden microphone. Next a taxi would appear and unload a citizen sporting dark glasses and a gray hat pulled low. The taxi driver, observant neighbors noted, was none other than Ivan Fedoseevich in disguise. As for his passenger—well, need we even ask?

Of all Kukusha's lovers, General Pobratimov was the most appreciative and lavish. Lately, though, he had not been able to do much: fallen into disfavor with the higher-ups, he had been removed for "Bonapartism" and sent off to command a remote military base, with a marshal's stars for consolation. But even in retreat he did not forget his friends: he helped get Tishka Kukushkin exempted from the army, and he fixed up Ivan Fedoseevich as military commissar of Moscow and facilitated his promotion to general.

Natasha Kukushkina, Yefim's daughter, had been working as an interpreter at Intourist and planned to go to graduate school, until she met a junior research fellow from the Meat and Dairy Industry Institute, one Semyon Zimmerman, and bore him a son. The baby, at the father's insistence, was named Ariel, in honor of (imagine!) the defense minister of Israel. Kukusha swore she would never acknowledge a grandson with such a name. She accepted the grandson eventually, but called him Artem.

The perfidious Zimmerman, meanwhile, was preparing an even more terrible blow for Kukusha. Natasha came home one day and announced that she and Senya (Zimmerman) had decided to move to their historic homeland, and she needed a certificate saying that her parents had no financial claims on her. Kukusha, horrified at this news, begged Natasha to come to her senses, to leave the cursed Zimmerman, to think of her baby. Kukusha reminded her daughter of all that she had done for her as a mother, of the gruel and cod-liver oil that had been fed her in childhood, of the Soviet regime that had given her an education, of the Komsomol that had nurtured her. She spoke of the terrors of capitalism, the Arabs, and the desert wind. She wept, took valerian drops, got down on her knees, threatened her daughter with terrible curses.

The certificate, of course, she refused to give. Not only that, she wrote to Intourist, the Meat and Dairy Industry Institute, the Visa and Registration Department, and her own Party organization, asking them to save her daughter from the toils of the Zionist conspiracy. But evidently the Zionists had infiltrated the Visa and Registration Department too, because in the end Natasha was allowed to leave without the certificate.

Kukusha came neither to the farewell party nor to the airport. Yefim said good-bye to his daughter secretly and thereafter concealed the fact that now and then he picked up letters from Israel at the central post office.

From the letters he learned that Natasha and her husband had settled well. Senya (now called Shimon) worked at a munitions factory and was drawing a decent salary, and she worked in a library. They had just one disappointment. Ariel, three-quarters Jewish and considered a Jew in the USSR, in Israel turned out to be not Jewish but Russian, since he was born of a Russian mother. (And his mother, who all her life had concealed her Jewishness, was now also a goy, for the same reason.)

Surprisingly, their daughter's departure had no effect at all on Yefim and Kukusha's situation. The Young Guard Publishing House continued to publish his novels about decent people, as if nothing had happened. Kukusha worked on her "No One and Nothing Is Forgotten," headed the Party committee, and wore her cross under her bra. Tishka was finishing graduate school.

Life went on.

Every morning Yefim is awakened by a soft thud. This is the newspaper falling: the elevator operator has put a copy of *Izvestia* through the slot in the door. There is supposed to be a mailbox inside, under the slot, but there isn't. Before Tishka was born, Yefim had meant to order the box, but never got around to it, and now there's no need. The thud of the paper falling is an excellent natural alarm clock for a light sleeper.

Yefim gets up. Wrapping his scrawny, hairy body in a green terry-cloth robe, he shuffles to the hall, picks up the paper, and takes it into the bathroom. After he's done in the bathroom, he goes to the kitchen to fix breakfast for Tishka. While the eggs are frying and the coffee is brewing and the bread and butter are being put on the table, a timer in Tishka's room turns on the Panasonic tape player, a gift from his parents. The sounds of rock music are muffled at first. Then a surge in volume—Tishka, on his way to the bathroom, has left his door open. The sound subsides—Tishka has shut himself up again, he's working out with his dumbbells. The music thunders again through the apartment—Tishka has gone to the shower, leaving his door open. Suddenly the music stops, and Tishka appears in the kitchen, washed, combed, and neatly dressed: Wrangler jeans, navy-blue Finnish blazer, white shirt, dark-red necktie.

"Morning, Papa!"

"Good morning!"

Tishka sits down to breakfast. Yefim watches his son with pleasure: tall and fair-haired, with Kukusha's gray eyes. Yefim has been lucky with his son. Tishka's an excellent student, doesn't drink, doesn't smoke, goes in for sports (tennis and karate). And he's always busy: a graduate student, member of the Student Science Society, member of the Komsomol committee at the institute, and president of the People's Patrol Council.

He eats his eggs, sips his coffee, scans the newspaper without interest. A reception at the Kremlin. A sowing campaign under way in Turkmenistan. The honor and conscience of a Party leader. Tension in the Persian Gulf. Sports, sports, sports . . .

"Will you be late tonight?" his father asks.

"Yes. We have a variety show, and then I'm on duty in the patrol."

"So we shouldn't expect you for supper?"

"No."

That's the entire conversation. Tishka leaves, and Yefim again brews coffee and fries eggs, this time for himself and Kukusha. When Kukusha leaves, he washes the dishes and goes to his desk to write his four pages—his daily average.

Yefim began work on a new novel—or, rather, he was about to begin, having just inserted a blank piece of Finnish paper (the Literary Fund had been giving it out recently) into the typewriter, and typing "Yefim Rakhlin" at the top and, under "Yefim Rakhlin," the title, *Operation!* He stopped to ponder the first sentence, which always gave him trouble.

The plot he had all thought out. The story (medical again) unfolds somewhere in the middle of the Pacific Ocean, on the research vessel *Galactica*. One of the crew members gets an attack of appendicitis. The patient needs an immediate appendectomy, but there is no one to do it except the ship's doctor, and *he* is the ship's doctor. Of course, when they learn what has happened, the decent people in Vladivostok and Moscow exchange radiograms and alert other ships' captains, who naturally all change course then and there and rush to the rescue. But, as in all Rakhlin novels, they are opposed by the forces of nature: gale, fog, freezing rain. In short, the sick doctor makes the only possible decision: makes the navigator his assistant, hands him a mirror, and performs the surgery himself.

Meanwhile, the decent people aren't just twiddling their thumbs. After much risk and travail, the *Glory,* the flagship of a whaling fleet, hauls alongside the *Galactica.* The flagship's doctor climbs up the rope ladder with his bag. But the operation is over.

"Well, colleague," says the doctor, examining the sutures, "the operation has been performed in accordance with all the rules of our venerable art. It remains only for me to congratulate you."

"Shh!" whispers the patient, putting a finger to his bloodless lips as he turns on the transistor radio on the night table beside him.

Today, it happens, is his birthday, and Radio Ocean, at his wife's request, is broadcasting the doctor's favorite love song: "We met, and in my lonely heart . . ."

After typing the title of the novel, *Operation!,* Yefim stopped to ponder. He pictured the word displayed vertically. The fact that his more recent novels all had titles consisting of only one word was no accident. Yefim had noticed that the popularization of literary works was greatly facilitated if the titles could be used in crossword puzzles. The puzzles were a form of free advertisement that had been scorned by those authors who gave their works such long and many-worded titles as *War and Peace* or *Crime and Punishment*. But some authors had been more farsighted, using titles like *Poltava, Oblomov,* or *Childhood*.

Yefim was proud of himself, that he had hit upon such a simple way to publicize his works. When, in crosswords printed in the *Evening News, Moscow Pravda,* or even *The Light,* he found that longed-for puzzle clue, "Novel by Y. Rakhlin," he would quickly count the number of letters and gleefully write in *avalanche*. Or *oiler*. The nine-letter *operation* would do nicely. In addition, you could make a rebus on it—and just then an excellent one occurred to him. Breathless with excitement, he wrote down the rebus on a piece of scrap paper and phoned Kukusha at work.

"What is it?" she asked.

"Listen, I have this great rebus. First, a woman holding a spear and singing, then a package of soldier's food, and the definition: a future novel by Rakhlin, in nine letters."

"Baldy, we're taping in five minutes."

"The first part," he said hastily, "is *opera*—"

"Baldy!" Kukusha shouted. "Fuck your goddamn opera! If you don't have anything to do, go out and get the milk!"

She often expressed herself this way. Yefim admired it, but couldn't do it himself.

He hung up and looked at the clock: a quarter past nine. Kostya Baranov might be awake by now, if he hadn't had too much to drink last night. Yefim dialed Kostya's number.

No one answered. He was about to hang up when he heard a click on the other end.

"Hello?" said a pained voice.

"I didn't wake you, did I?" asked Yefim.

"Of course you woke me."

"Sorry. I just wanted to try a rebus on you."

"A rebus."

"A good one. The first half of the word is a woman with a spear, singing, in five letters. The second half is a package of soldier's food, six letters. Put together, it's a nine-letter word for surgery."

"Listen, old man, I may have had a drop too much at the Literary Club last night, but you weren't drinking. And your arithmetic's weak. Five and six don't make nine."

Smiling into the receiver, Yefim explained that rebus had overlapping. "The first part is *opera,* see. The second part is *ration*. The last syllable of the first word is the first syllable of the last word. It's the title of my new novel."

"You're writing another novel?" Kostya asked.

"I am," Yefim admitted smugly.

"Wonderful," Kostya said with a yawn. "No work stoppages for you. You write faster than I read."

"And by the way," Yefim asked, "did you read *Avalanche!*?"

"*Avalanche*. What's *Avalanche*?"

"My novel. The one I gave you last week."

"Oh, that," Kostya said. "Why do you ask?"

"I'd like to know your opinion of it."

"My opinion is always extremely negative."

"Did you read it?"

"Of course not."

"Then how can you judge it?"

"Old man, if someone gives me a piece of rotten meat, one bite is enough. I don't have to eat the whole thing."

This was not their first such exchange. Yefim, as usual, got angry and began shouting that Kostya was a boor, knew nothing about literature, and had no idea how much fan mail Yefim got. Why, he'd got a letter just yesterday from a woman who wrote that her whole family had read *Avalanche!,* had read it together, and it had brought tears to her eyes.

"Here, listen." The letter lay open before him and Yefim pulled it closer. " 'Your book, in its humanistic zeal and romantic spirit, is not like those novels one so frequently encounters nowadays, filled with plausible but boring descriptions of life, with uninspired characters, their earthbound dreams and petty cares. It acquaints us with real heroes, whose example we want to follow. Thank you, dear Comrade Rakhlin, for being as you are.' "

"God!" Kostya groaned into the receiver. "What a character! She's retired, I'll bet. Member of the Communist Party since year one."

He was right. The reader had signed herself "N. Kruglova, Retired on Special Pension, Member of the Communist Party since 1927." But Yefim did not tell him this.

"I can't talk with you," he said. "You don't understand a thing." And he slammed down the receiver.

His mood was spoiled. He didn't feel like writing anymore. The idea for *Operation!,* which had come so easily, no longer gave him joy. The last episode, though, where the doctor listens to his favorite song—that still seemed good.

"Fool," Yefim said, addressing Kostya. "I've written eleven books. How many have you written?"

Not a hard question to answer, that, because in his whole life Kostya Baranov had written just one book, a novella. It had got him accepted into the Writers' Union and had been reprinted three times, but he had not been able to produce anything else. He made his living by reviewing for the Military Publishing House and doing short scripts at the People's Science Film Studio.

But Yefim was as angry with himself as he was with Kostya. Why did he allow his friend to treat him this way? Why did he put up with his insults and abuse? Because he did put up with them. Sometimes Yefim would get into a long argument defending the value of his writing—and Kostya would suggest that he look in the mirror or compare what he wrote with Chekhov's prose.

Kostya was right about the mirror. Sometimes Yefim went to the big pier glass that stood in the hall and stared long at his reflection. He saw a pathetic, lop-eared, wrinkled face with small features and billiard-ball pate, in the middle of which curled one loose kinky strand of hair. And he saw large, prominent, Jewish eyes filled with a meaningless sorrow.

As for Chekhov, Yefim read him often and closely. And didn't understand a thing. Each time he read Chekhov, he . . . he would never confess this to anyone, of course, but ever . . . but each time he read Chekhov, he felt that there was really nothing special about the writing. He, Yefim Rakhlin, wrote just as well. Perhaps even a little better.

Yefim paced the room nervously, angrily. He waved his arms, muttered, made faces. Sometimes, even, like a royal guardsman of old (an odd atavism, this, incompatible with his origins), he drew himself up, clicked his heels (though wearing floppy slippers), gave a sharp nod, and said through his teeth, "Never, sir!" And he spat in the face of his imaginary opponent, that is Kostya Baranov.

His friendship with Kostya made no sense. He was forced to agree with Kukusha, who had never understood what bound the two. "He loves me," Yefim would tell her, though not sure he believed that. But whether he believed that or not, he and Kostya did have something like love between them. If not love, an attachment. Neither of them—despite the constant exchange of insults and reproaches—could go a single day without the other. As if the insults and reproaches were necessary.

Yefim would have to sever all relations with Kostya. Yes, he had made up his mind (as he had made up his mind a thousand times before) and immediately felt relieved. He was not alone, after all. He had his beloved wife; he had his beloved son; he had his beloved albeit prodigal daughter. She had left, but she was still his daughter. She wrote, he wrote. And there was that inexhaustible source of torment and joy—his work.

He sat at his typewriter again. He had only to put together the first sentence, and after that the book would write itself. So what if they said he wasn't a great writer? What did great mean? Nothing. Anyway, Yefim enjoyed writing, and even if they didn't publish him and pay him he would write, he would write for the sheer pleasure of it. They did publish him, though, and in large printings, and paid him well. He had never had so much money. When he had worked as a rank-and-file staff writer for the journal *Geology and Mineralogy,* he had made only a fraction of his present salary, and had had to listen to his boss's reprimands whenever he was late, and to ask permission every time he needed to go to the clinic or the store.

The first sentence—once it was written, descriptions of nature would follow, people would appear, they would enter into relationships, and the mysterious process of creation, not given to many to experience, would begin.

Regaining his composure, Yefim typed:

> Captain Kolomiytsev stood on the bridge, casting a dreary eye on the raging storm. Towering waves loomed and hurled themselves, one after the another, at the mighty breast of the ship like desperate kamikazis . . .

The simile pleased Yefim, but suddenly he had doubts about the spelling of kamikaze. Was it *kamikazi* or *kamekazi*? He pulled the telephone over and began dialing Kostya's number, but then remembered his decision.

No sooner did he put down the receiver than the phone

rang. You could always tell who was calling by the way the phone rang. A boss's ring was loud, abrupt. Someone asking you a favor—lilting, ingratiating. This ring was lax, insolent.

"Well, what is it now?" Yefim asked, picking up the receiver.

"Listen," Kostya lisped. "I completely forgot to tell you. They're giving hats to the writers."

"I see," Yefim said, and hung up. He did not hang up in anger; it was for another reason.

Yefim and Kostya, living at a considerable distance from each other, did most of their socializing on the phone. On the phone they discussed their problems, items of news, rumors about this or that colleague, the next conference in the prose section, who had been caught embezzling what from where, whose wife had left whom for whom, not to mention politics. They criticized the collective farm system, the censors, a book by the First Secretary of the Writers' Union. They dealt with the events in the Near East, the defection of yet another KGB agent to the West, the declaration by a new dissident group. The latest thing reported on the BBC.

But, in case anyone listened in, and that was to be expected, they had developed over the years an elaborate system of code words. If, for example, Yefim told Kostya that according to Brother Boris in London they would be getting a large shipment of aperitifs, Kostya knew immediately that aperitifs meant operatives and Brother Boris meant the BBC, that, in other words, a large group of Soviet spies was being expelled from England. Both, of course, were gladdened by this news, as they were gladdened by any embarrassment or setback to the state, the same state for which the heroes of Yefim's books risked their lives and were even willing to part with various body parts. Or if, for another example, Kostya called and said he had some fresh veal for him, Yefim immediately ran out, grabbed a taxi, and set off for the distant sticks of Belyaevo-Bogorodskoe—not because his mouth watered for a chop or a roast. No, the desired object was a book, Solzhenitsyn's *The Oak and the Calf*.

So when Kostya said that the writers were getting hats, Yefim was quick to hang up—to avoid undue attention from an eavesdropper and so he could think what the words *writers* and *hats* were supposed to mean.

It probably had to do with the group of economists who recently wrote an open letter demanding a bolder expansion of the private sector. The letter had found its way to the West, had been broadcast by the BBC, Voice of America, German Wave, Liberty, and Radio Canada. Now these "writers" were being "handed their hats." Yefim, wanting to learn the details, glanced at his watch. Still too early. The stations he listened to were on the air only in the evening, and Radio Liberty, which operated around the clock, couldn't be heard in his neighborhood.

Evening was too long to wait. Forgetting his decision, he telephoned Kostya.

"About those hats," he asked, "are they giving them out soon?"

"Not that soon. They're sewing them to order," Kostya said.

"Actually sewing them!" Yefim cried, appalled that the "writers" would be "sewn up," that is, put in prison.

"Why are you so surprised?" Kostya asked. "Didn't

you hear at the last meeting when Lukin said we should take better care of our writers? They're building a new writers' lodge in Sochi, the clinic has introduced a course in physical fitness, and the Literary Fund is taking orders for hats. I was there yesterday, and I ordered a nice one for myself, in gray rabbit, with earflaps."

"So you . . . were talking about ordinary winter hats?" Yefim asked cautiously.

"I suppose, if you liked, you could have them make you a summer hat."

For no reason at all, Yefim got angry. "And for hats you had to call me in the morning!" he shouted. "You know that the morning's my best time for working!"

He slammed down the receiver, but a minute later picked it up again and dialed Kostya.

"Sorry I blew up."

"Nerves. I understand," Kostya said magnanimously. "Incidentally, the clinic has a new psychiatrist, Dr. Berkovich—board-certified."

Yefim let the dig pass and asked what, exactly, Kostya knew about the hats. Kostya told him that the Literary Fund's board of directors had decided to make hats for writers in accordance with their importance. Reindeer fawn for the foremost writers, muskrat for the leading, marmot for the outstanding . . .

"You understand, of course," Kostya said, "that the foremost writers are the secretaries of the National Writers' Union. The leading are the secretaries of the Writers' Union of the Russian Republic. And the outstanding are the secretaries of the Moscow Writers'

Union, though among their number there may be one or two who aren't secretaries, merely writers."

"Like you and me," Yefim said, smiling into the receiver.

"You and me? Oh, come, we're not writers. We're just members of the Writers' Union. Writers, they're a different breed altogether. They'll be given something like fox or marten (I really don't know furs). As for you and me—rabbit. Rabbit fits our rank."

Yes, that was indeed how the hierarchy looked. Still, in putting himself on a level with Yefim, Kostya had gone too far. But Yefim said nothing, because on the whole Kostya was right. Yefim may have written eleven books, but even if he had written a hundred and eleven, he would still be put at the bottom of the totem pole. Still be given the worst rooms at the writers' lodges, denied a subscription to the magazine *America,* and not have his photograph appear on his birthday. As for the hat, well, of course he would get the cheapest.

But this had its advantages: no one would envy him, no one would covet his place, and he could quietly continue to turn out novels about decent people.

So Yefim did not argue with Kostya. Let those who had nothing better to do fight for the hats. He had his own hat, of wolf fur; the reindeer breeders had given it to him last year.

He hung up, carried the phone to the other room, and covered it with a pillow so he could work undisturbed. But when he returned to the typewriter, a fit of rage overcame him and he began banging away at the keys without stopping to think. This is what he wrote:

The LitFund is giving hats to the writers. Fine, wonderful, but I don't need one, I have my own hat. It's a good hat, a wolf fur, warm, soft. I don't need another hat. Let others fight for hats, not me, I have better things to do. Besides, I already have a hat, a wolf fur, warm, and it's a good hat. You can keep your hats, gentlemen, you can eat them, and if you can't eat them, I hope you choke on them.

Rereading what he had written, he was amazed. This had happened before to him—writing in a frenzy. But usually it bore some relation to the story at hand. Here, the result was nonsense. Pursing his lips in perplexity, Yefim shook his head and stuck the page under the pile of old rough drafts that lay to the right of his typewriter. (The page was subsequently found and read. It moved the critic Sorokin to say that Rakhlin's talent had not been properly appreciated.) Unaware that he had done something talented, Yefim inserted a fresh sheet and again addressed himself to Captain Kolomiytsev, who was standing in a stiff wind, his hand clutching his hat to keep it from flying off.

Yefim noticed that he had written the word *hat* again. Angry, he replaced it with a cap with a faded gold anchor.

Captain Kolomiytsev, then, stood in a stiff wind, his hand clutching his cap with a faded gold anchor. Much better. But now Yefim had to bring in the main hero, the ship's doctor. It so happened that the doctor passed by the captain at that moment (Yefim didn't have a reason yet, but he would come up with one).

"Doctor!" the captain hailed him.

"At your service, sir!" the doctor replied, politely tipping his hat.

"Pah!" Yefim spat, and hit his knee in irritation. Why all these hats?

He tore up this sheet and was about to insert another when he heard the muffled ring of the telephone in the next room.

"Listen," Kostya said, "I read your *Avalanche!* It's brilliant."

Never before had Kostya said such a thing. Yefim was flabbergasted. He did not know what to say. Suspecting a trick, he asked Kostya what he meant.

"Your novel *Avalanche!* is brilliant," Kostya repeated.

"But just twenty minutes ago, you said you hadn't read it."

"But just twenty minutes ago I hadn't, but now I have."

"Kostya," Yefim groaned, "please, let me alone. You know I work in the mornings." *Unlike some,* he could have added, but didn't.

"All right. I just thought you'd like to hear my opinion. The novel is brilliant . . ."

Brilliant had such an alluring sound that Yefim could not hang up.

". . . though a little long-winded," Kostya went on.

"Long-winded? Why long-winded?"

"Well, let's analyze it. Take the beginning: 'The day was hot. Savely Morgunov sat at his desk and watched a fly beat against the windowpane.' Stunning!"

"It *is* pretty good," Yefim admitted bashfully.

"Not pretty good," Kostya insisted. "Stunning! Though obscure."

"Obscure?"

"Very obscure."

This pleased Yefim, who in his heart of hearts had always wanted to write something obscure or even impenetrable.

"Picture it, " Kostya continued. "The height of summer, the sun at the zenith, the heat unbearable, and the windows all closed. Savely sits, and the fly beats against the windowpane. He's hot, exhausted. He watches the fly and thinks that he, the fly, is beating helplessly against the windowpane. Hopelessly. He sits in the heat and sweats, and the fly beats against the windowpane. This Savely, by the way—what is he?"

"A construction boss," Yefim said warily.

"I thought as much. All the better. The heat is sweltering, the fly beats, the construction boss sweats. Materials are short, the workers are drunk, his supervisor hurls four-letter words at him, the quota will never be met. The construction boss sweats, his mood is dark, the fly beats against the windowpane. He realizes that his life is a failure, his job is a farce, his wife is hysterical, his son is shooting up, and his daughter's a whore."

"What!?" Yefim squealed. "What are you talking about? I don't have drug addicts and whores in my books!"

"It doesn't matter whether or not you have drug addicts and whores in your books. This is where my thoughts, my imagination leads me. You have to trust the reader. You have to give him rein. That's why I said the book is long-winded. Why write six hundred pages when the whole thing's clear from the first line?"

"Nothing's clear to you!" Yefim cried shrilly. "I only write about decent people. Indecent people don't interest me. And anyway, the construction boss is a bachelor."

"Ah, a homosexual!" Kostya said. "That's different, then. Everything takes on a different meaning. He sits, he sweats, the fly beats against the windowpane . . ."

Yefim couldn't stand it. He slammed down the receiver.

He was going to remove the phone again, but it started ringing in his hands.

"Baldy," said the receiver in Kukusha's voice, "I forgot to tell you. Don't go anywhere before lunch. They're bringing the clothes back from the laundry."

"Right," Yefim said.

The shortness of his reply surprised Kukusha. "The receipt's on the table in front of the mirror," she said just to say something.

"Right."

"Baldy," she asked, "is anything wrong?"

"No."

"Bullshit. I can tell by your voice, you aren't yourself. What happened?"

Yefim was always scrupulously polite, even ingratiating, when he spoke to his wife. But now he lost his temper. "Nothing happened, nothing!" he shouted tearfully. "Everything's just fine. Savely's fine, the fly is fine, and the Literary Fund is giving out hats."

After a pause, Kukusha said, "Baldy, you haven't gone crazy, have you?"

Yefim got a grip on himself. "Maybe. I'm sorry. It's all Kostya's fault."

"I thought as much. What did he tell you?"

"Nothing, really. I don't feel like talking about it. The LitFund is making hats for the writers."

And he told her, smiling now, what he had heard from Kostya, the giving of hats according to importance: reindeer fawn for the foremost writers, muskrat for the leading, marmot for the outstanding . . .

"And rabbit," he said, "for me."

"Why only rabbit?" Kukusha asked, not amused.

He repeated Kostya's argument.

"That's nonsense," she said. "Kostya, maybe, deserves rabbit, he's a do-nothing and a lush to boot. But you, you're a working writer. You travel on assignment, meet important people—you can't go around in a rabbit hat!"

"Why get upset? I don't have to wear a rabbit hat, I have a hat, a good hat, wolf fur, it's warm."

Kukusha answered with silence. She always did this when she wanted to express displeasure.

"Now, Kukusha, sweetie, don't be mad," Yefim said, cringing. "I'll go put my name in, if you want. But it won't help. You know I'm not a secretary of the Writers' Union. I'm not a Party member. And I have a slight problem in the ethnic origin area."

"Well, if you feel that way about it—that you're inferior—then there's no reason to go. You're insignificant, a nothing, and anyway you have your own hat, don't you? You also happen to have a family, and a grown son, and *his* hat is threadbare, he's worn it for two years now. But why talk to you! You're always so polite, smiling at everyone, bowing, you don't need anything, you're so good, you bastard!"

A dial tone—Kukusha had hung up on him.

Yefim smiled to himself, putting down the receiver. Women were so illogical. How could he be good and at the same time a bastard?

But maybe she was right, after all. Maybe he was too good. What use was his great modesty? He recalled his length of service as a writer, the number of books he'd written, and the pensioner Mrs. Kruglova's letter.

With a sigh, he took the page with the unfinished description of Captain Kolomiytsev out of the typewriter (it looked as if he wouldn't get much done today) and quickly composed a letter of appreciation. He enumerated his eighteen years, eleven books, and government decorations, then added that he often went on distant assignments, including the regions of the Far North (where a hat must be warm), and met with people of fearless professions as well as local leaders (so the hat should be worthy of a writer from the capital). For good measure, he mentioned his tireless community work—as a member of the Commission on Adventure Literature.

The application filled a whole page and concluded with a request that they "accept an order for headgear made of . . ." Here he stopped. He couldn't put down a fur reserved for the foremost, leading, or outstanding, and on the other hand he didn't want to limit the authorities' choice to marmot, so he wrote vaguely, ". . . of quality fur."

Before Yefim set out for the Literary Fund co-op, he received a visit from the fairy-tale writer Solomon Yevseevich Fishkin, who lived two floors below. Fishkin came up in his pajamas and slippers to ask for a cigarette, to try out the plot of a fairy tale, and to share information about the trials of their neighbor Vaska Tryoshkin, poet, and defender of the Russian national character against chemistry and Jews.

Vaska was a tall, thin, morose man. His moroseness was caused by the fact that he felt he was surrounded (and he was indeed) by members of an ethnic group repugnant to him. Above him lived Rakhlin, below him Fishkin, on his left the literary critic Axelrod, on his right Professor Blok. Try as he might, Vaska could not understand how it happened that in the Soviet Union the Jews (so his friend Cherpakov told him) were between six- and seven-tenths of a percent of the population as a whole, while here in the writers' building he, a lone Russian, found himself in close proximity to four Jews. In this cooperative apartment building (he had calculated it many times) and probably in the whole Writers' Union, the Jews constituted no less than eighty percent—a statistic that plunged Vaska into near despair.

Considering it his moral obligation to guard Russia from what he referred to in private as universal Hebraization (but in print, Zionization), Vaska sounded the alarm. He wrote letters to the Communist Party Central Committee, the Presidium of the Supreme Soviet of the USSR, the Writers' Union, the Academy of Sciences, and the newspapers. The occasional answers he received were evasive. Sometimes people called him in, chatted, and expressed sympathy, but at the same time reminded him of certain principles of our land: brotherly internationalism and a tolerance even toward pernicious ethnic groups.

The government's tolerance, in Vaska's opinion, had gone too far. The Jews (Zionists) with the aid of their Yid-Freemason sympathizers (Cherpakov's phrase) had already seized key positions throughout the world and in our nation. Jews were elected as presidents and prime ministers, and leaders of other ethnic origins were made to marry Jewish women. Daily and hourly, the Jews were enmeshing the planet in the web of their universal plot.

Vaska saw signs of this plot everywhere. In the evening, when he looked up at the sky, the stars formed cabalistic Zionist figures and winked at one another. There were secret Zionist symbols in the design of the buildings and the layout of the streets. Flipping through newspapers and magazines, Vaska found six-pointed stars, Zionist watermarks, and linguistic sabotage. In one column, for example, would be the headline "A Russian Song Festival," and in the column to the left, at the same level, the headline of an international article, "We Will Never Allow," thus creating the message: "We Will Never Allow a Russian Song Festival."

Reporting all this to the authorities, Vaska understood how dangerous was the path he had embarked on. The Zionists, in an effort to get rid of him, were poisoning him with odorless gases and invisible rays. This was why his wife had come down with cancer, and why he suffered from headaches and premature ejaculation. To protect himself, Vaska always sniffed his food, boiled his water, and put lead foil in his underpants. Recently he had informed the Central Committee, the KGB, and the Writers' Union about the mysterious disappearance of his cat. The Zionists, he was convinced, had stolen her. He received no answer.

The door of the Rakhlins' apartment was open. Walking in, Fishkin caught Yefim in front of the mirror. The novelist had on a sheepskin coat, and over his head he held a blue denim cap in one hand and a fur hat (wolf) in the other.

"Yefim," his neighbor said in surprise, "what is this? You think maybe you have two heads?"

The fairy-tale writer's perplexity was soon dispelled, however. Yefim explained the situation and his predicament. He didn't know which to wear: in the denim cap he didn't look respectable, and they might refuse him for that reason, but if he wore, instead, the wolf fur, they might refuse him because he already had a hat.

"People have completely taken leave of their senses," said Fishkin, shaking his head. "Twenty phone calls I've had already about these hats. Everyone's mad at the LitFund. You want my advice? Here's my advice: Go without a hat. You look respectable in your sheepskin coat. No one will think that you don't have a hat, but on the other hand, no one will conclude that you don't need a hat." He thought a moment and added, "Even so, they won't give you anything good."

"And why won't they?" Yefim asked in exasperation. "Why should they give you a hat and not me?"

"No, Yefim, they treat us more fairly than you suppose. They won't give me one either. And the reason is, we're both ugly ducklings. Incidentally, I've thought of a new fairy tale on that theme. Would you like to hear it?"

Yefim was in no mood to hear a fairy tale, but he couldn't very well say no to the old man. "Go ahead. But make it quick, because I don't have time."

"You'll like it," Fishkin promised. "The title is 'The Return of the Ugly Duckling.' Good, isn't it?"

"A good title," Yefim said, "should be one word."

Fishkin nodded. "Then we'll call it 'Return.' So listen. The Ugly Duckling, persecuted by his comrades, leaves them and goes to live on a small, deserted lake. There he grows into a Beautiful Swan. Discovering this, he rejoices and decides to return on his own, to show everyone. He's ready to forgive his comrades for the insults of the past. But they greet him with even greater contempt than before. You see, while he was away, they began to call themselves swans. And established a swan pecking order. The post of Beautiful Swan is occupied by a drake who thinks he's big but actually is only fat. And there are two Foremost Swans, four Leading, and sixteen Outstanding. The rest are rank-and-file swans."

"Is this about the Writers' Union?" Yefim asked.

"Why does everything have to be about your stinking union?" Fishkin said indignantly, as though he himself did not belong to it. "It's about people in general. But back to the story. When he hears all this, the Beautiful Swan says, 'All right. I'm not ambitious. I don't mind being like everyone else. I'll be a rank-and-file swan.' At that, the ducks laugh scornfully. 'What a nerve!' they say. 'All our lives we struggle to be swans, and he wants to receive the title for nothing!' And some of the ducks say he's suffering from delusions of grandeur. But then they put their heads together and reconsider. After all, he is their own kind, a web-foot. They reflect and decide to grant him the position of Ugly Duckling—"

"With a period of probation!" Yefim said, chuckling.

"Exactly." Fishkin smiled.

"And he agrees?"

"That I haven't figured out yet," Fishkin said. "He probably doesn't. He probably returns to his lake, swims around there, looks at his reflection, and tells himself, though without conviction, 'I look more like a swan than they do.' "

"And the ducks?"

"They are silent on the subject. They want to forget about the swan, they pretend he doesn't exist. Because if he does exist, then they have to call themselves something else, not swans."

After telling Yefim about Vaska Tryoshkin's lost cat, Fishkin bummed two cigarettes (one for an emergency) and shuffled downstairs to his apartment. Shortly thereafter, Yefim appeared in a sheepskin coat, a red muffler, and with his head bare. Standing slightly at an angle because of the weight of his bulging attaché case, he pressed the elevator button. As he waited for the elevator, he thought about the tale he had just heard. And was not he, too, a persecuted Beautiful Swan?

The elevator arrived with a thud and a scrape. Two floors down, Yefim realized that he had forgotten the laundry receipt. This unnerved him, because he believed superstitiously that if you forgot something, your trip wouldn't be successful. He stopped the elevator and went back up, got the receipt, but then looked in the mirror before going out again. In the mirror he saw not a Beautiful Swan but an Aging Sad Man of Jewish Appearance who, moreover, was toothless. Yefim had also forgotten his teeth. While he was putting his teeth in and clicking them in front of the mirror, someone appropriated the elevator. Yefim, deciding not to wait, took the stairs.

As he passed Vaska's apartment, the brown Leatherette-covered door opened slightly. In the crack burned the poet's suspicious eye. "Where's he going? And why without a hat?" Vaska wondered.

Yefim noticed his neighbor's eye. He was reluctant to greet him, but nevertheless said hello, submitting to his innate good breeding, and raised his hand to touch his hat. But he touched his bare forehead. He retreated in confusion, smiling foolishly at the poet. Vaska closed the door without a word, went to his study, and made the following entry in a special notebook with an oilcloth cover: "Today at 11:45, the Zionist Rakhlin on the stairs (despite the fact that the elevator is working!!), with a large attaché case and no hat."

Ordinarily the elevator attendant sat with her knitting in her place downstairs by the public telephone, but now she was not there. Yefim saw her, instead, in the courtyard. She was running around, agitated.

"What nerve!" she shouted, addressing the whole courtyard. "No shame! I should call the police!"

"Varvara Grigorevna, what happened?" Yefim asked.

"What happened? I was never so furious in my life! The stink they made! Drunken bums! On their way to the metro, they all, every one of them, turn in here and piss under the archway. I told them: 'Citizens, what do you think you're doing? Where do you think you're pissing? This is not a toilet! People live here—writers. If you have to piss, piss across the street!' And the police don't care. I've told the officer I don't know how many times. 'It's embarrassing,' I told him. 'And *writers* live here. It's not like it's you and me.' But he—Yefim Semyonovich, what's wrong with you?" she cried. "What are you doing, out in such weather without a hat? You'll catch a cold in your head. And it's not like your head's the same as ours. Ours one could use to drive nails. But you need yours for your work."

"Never mind, Varvara Grigorevna. We have to harden ourselves," Yefim replied briskly. He gave her the laundry receipt and walked on. The temperature wasn't really that low. But there was a wind, and his bald pate, not accustomed to being bare, was soon freezing.

Walking out through the gate, Yefim immediately became part of the constant, disorderly flow of people and vehicles sloshing through the gray mix of snow and salt. The kiosks that stood opposite the apartment house and near the entrance to the metro all had long lines of people waiting patiently, shifting from foot to foot and breathing steam. There was a line for deluxe ice cream in forty-eight-kopeck packets, another for Hungarian peas in glass jars, a third for Treasures, cigarettes from Bulgaria. The fourth line, curving, was at the stop for the microbus that shuttled between the airport metro station and the Leningrad Road Farmers' Market.

The lobby of the co-op was noisier than usual. Several people were pressed around a small desk, where a mustached brunette, Serafima Borisovna, was taking an order for carbon paper and East German typewriter ribbons. The poet and songwriter Samarin was showing off a new suit to his round young wife. Feet wide apart, he stood in the middle of the lobby wearing a jacket bristling with pins, a huge fox-fur hat perched uncertainly on his head like a burnt haystack. Crawling anxiously back and forth between Samarin's legs was the robust and red-faced tailor Sanya Zarubin, a measuring tape around his neck. The hum of conversations was periodically drowned out by a dreadful squealing from the basement, where Arkasha Glotov, a sewing machine operator, was grinding porcelain dentures, which he did, of course, "on the side," illegally.

Though he was fully stocked with carbons, typewriter ribbons, and even Finnish paper, Yefim elbowed his way to Serafima Borisovna and handed her a Guardsman chocolate bar from his attaché case. From her he learned that the orders for the hats were being processed personally by the director, one Andrey Andreevich Shchupov, a new man, strict and principled. "Strict and principled" meant he didn't take bribes, or at least didn't take them indiscriminately—unlike the old director, whose downfall, indeed, had been that he took bribes from everyone. The old director hadn't fallen very far, however; he had been transferred to the post of director of a writers' lodge outside Moscow, where, again, he didn't live on his salary alone.

The line to see the director began here in the lobby and stretched down the corridor to a black door.

"Who's here for reindeer fawn?" Yefim joked.

The last in line was the humorist Yerofeev, a dour older man with a scar on his left cheek.

"For fawn, my friend, one does not stand in line," he lectured. "Fawn is brought to one's house with a thank you and a bow. It is for more common fur that one stands in line."

Yefim noticed that the writers in line had also given thought to their headgear. Some, like him, wore none. Others wore denim caps. In his hands Yerofeev held a policeman's hat with a star. The ratteen overcoat he wore was unbuttoned to reveal a long dark jacket with two rows of medals. "What a fool I am!" Yefim thought. He shouldn't have written about his decorations, he should have pinned them on. It would have made a better impression.

He took his place behind the humorist. Not to waste time, he took a copy of *Avalanche!* from his attaché case, opened it on his knee, and boldly inscribed on the title page, "To Andrey Andreevich Shchupov, as a token of deep respect. Y. Rakhlin."

"What's the date today?" he asked Yerofeev, and as he filled in the date he heard his nickname: "Fima!"

He looked around and saw, sitting at a magazine table by the window, his old classmate from the literary institute, the prose writer Anatoly Mylnikov, in a heavy fur coat, unbuttoned. Mylnikov's face was red, as if he'd come from the public bath; his temples glistened with sweat, and a grayish lock of hair had twisted into a curl and stuck to his forehead.

"I didn't notice you," Yefim apologized. "Have you come for a hat, too?"

"No." Mylnikov frowned. "I have my own, here." He indicated the hat that lay in his lap. "It's badger. Some writer alcoholic promised me imported faucets for my bathroom, so here I am, waiting. Have a seat."

"I thought you'd come for a hat," Yefim said, sitting down with a sigh. "I have a hat, too, wolf, a gift from the reindeer breeders. But if they're giving them away, why not take one?"

"Oh, you mean the hats they make here. I got mine a couple of months ago. Gave it to my nephew. When he saw that muskrat, he took a fancy to it."

"They gave you muskrat?" Yefim asked in surprise.

"Yes, muskrat. Why?"

"Oh, nothing," Yefim said, lowering his eyes. "They gave Kostya Baranov rabbit. But you . . . you're a living classic."

Mylnikov's career had blossomed where Yefim's had not, even though Mylnikov didn't write much about decent people, didn't write a lot, and was more panned than praised by the press. But Mylnikov's books, panned, attracted attention and had been translated into several languages, and the authorities had to reckon with this. Mylnikov continued to be published and was even allowed abroad, both as a member of various delegations and as an individual. Observing Mylnikov's career, Yefim concluded that occasionally provoking official displeasure could prove advantageous, as long as you knew how to keep your balance. Recognition from the critics actually meant nothing: you were praised, but you were despised.

On his foreign royalties Mylnikov had bought himself an export-grade Volga (other writers drove Zhigulis, at best) and a videotape recorder. At home he treated his guests to whiskey and gin.

Now he was telling Yefim about his recent trip to London, where he had delivered a couple of lectures, given interviews, seen the latest porno masterpiece, and even appeared on the BBC. He had been, he said, a howling success in London.

"The *Times* called me a modern Chekhov," Mylnikov confided. "And the *Guardian* had a very favorable review . . ."

He was about to produce the review and read it, but Yefim's turn came. He was summoned in to see the director.

Entering the director's office, Yefim saw behind the heavy desk and beneath the poster with Politburo portraits, a man with a wooden face.

"Greetings, Andrey Andreevich!" Yefim exclaimed cheerfully, bobbing his head to present an image of natural, easy, open affability. But under the director's heavy gaze he shriveled, and felt his face crinkle into a miserable, servile smile.

The director said nothing.

Listing to one side under the weight of his attaché

case and feeling an awful fidgetiness throughout his body, Yefim advanced toward the desk, smiling and bowing absurdly as he walked.

"Yefim Semyonovich Rakhlin," he said, and looked at the director with the hope that the director now would introduce himself. But Andrey Andreevich only stared at Yefim. He did not answer, did not rise, did not shake hands, did not even invite him to sit down.

Usually co-op supervisors were more polite to writers.

Without an invitation, then, Yefim pulled up a chair, sat down, put his attaché case on his lap, and, regaining some of his composure, smiled ingratiatingly at Andrey Andreevich. "So you will be our new director?"

"Not will be. Am," Andrey Andreevich said.

"Oh, yes, yes, of course." Yefim nodded hastily. "Not *will be,* but *are,* I expressed myself incorrectly. So, you've probably come to us from the retail area?"

Andrey Andreevich studied Yefim for a moment in silence, then said, "No. I'm from the security system."

To this reply Yefim's own system reacted with a sudden drop in temperature and a downward plunge as well, in the pit of his stomach. Not that he was frightened (there was no reason for fear), but he twitched unnaturally and looked down. Then he raised his head and fastened his gaze on the director, giving him to understand that he had nothing, absolutely nothing, to hide from the security system, that he was clean as the proverbial whistle. But, encountering the director's heavy stare, he paled and dropped his eyes again. He couldn't help it. And so Yefim gave himself away, for one who is whistle-clean has no need to avert his eyes.

"From the System!" he repeated heartily. "Pleased to

meet you!" With his whole being he wanted to express respect for the director's former job, but he couldn't control his shifting eyes. "So, they sent you here to reinforce us?"

"Yes. What can I do for you?"

Confused, quailing, no longer even attempting to make eye contact, Yefim hastily began to explain that he had heard that one could order a hat made at the LitFund, and a hat was exactly what he needed. He needed, moreover, a good hat, since he often went on expeditions of the highest national and scientific nature during which expeditions he studied the life of our fearless compatriots.

Andrey Andreevich asked Yefim if he was a member of the Writers' Union. Yefim replied that he had been a member for eighteen years now, that he had been given his card by Konstantin Fedin personally, and that he, Rakhlin, was a war veteran, possessed government decorations, had written eleven books, and took an active part in the Commission on Adventure Literature. Then he put his application on the desk. The director scanned the page, opened a desk drawer, and stared into it for a long time, working his lips. Then the drawer was slid shut with a bang, and words appeared on Yefim's application, slantwise, in red pencil. Yefim picked up the application, got to his feet, slapped his pockets, took out his glasses, fastened them on, and read: "Accept an order, fur hat, domestic tomcat, medium fluffy."

"Domestic tomcat," Yefim said uncertainly. "What is that?"

"You've never seen a cat?" It was the director's turn to be surprised.

"Well, of course . . . a cat . . . I've seen cats in general. My neighbor had a cat that recently disappeared. But making hats out of cats . . . I didn't know they did that, to tell the truth. Excuse me, I'm not well-informed: is cat fur considered better quality than rabbit, or worse?"

"Worse, I would think," the director said indifferently. "Rabbits have to be raised, but cats breed by themselves."

Then he stared into space, waiting for his visitor to leave.

His visitor, however, did not leave. His visitor stood stunned. He had come to ask for something better than rabbit, and they were giving him worse. Now he had to petition for rabbit, though rabbit did not suit him at all.

"Allow me . . ." Yefim began, distraught. "I don't quite understand. If cat is inferior to rabbit, then why do I get cat? I'm a veteran. I have medals. Eighteen years in the Writers' Union. I've written eleven books."

"Eleven, that's good," was all the director said.

"But yesterday, Konstantin Baranov was in to see you. He's a member of the Writers' Union too, although he's written only one book, not eleven. Him you put down for rabbit. Why does Baranov get rabbit, and I tomcat?"

"I don't know who Baranov is or what I put him down for. I have three lists of writers, and you aren't on any of them. For people who fall outside the list, all I have is cat fur. That's it."

Yefim tried to convince the director that his name had been omitted from the lists as a result of some misunderstanding or error. He mentioned, again, his length of service, the number of books he had published, his military past. But Andrey Andreevich folded his arms on his chest, waiting for his visitor to talk himself out and leave.

When he saw that the director was deaf to all entreaty, Yefim made a pitiful face and refused to take back his application. Muttering a meaningless threat that he would complain, he started for the door. But he grasped the knob, he remembered something. He had committed a great oversight, which he must correct at once.

He returned to the director's desk, and his expression, as he walked, was transformed from pitiful to kind or even magnanimous. But there was still pathos in Yefim's face as he drew a copy of *Avalanche!* from his attaché case and laid the imitation leather volume on the desk in front of the director.

"I completely forgot," he said, smiling and nodding. "This is for you."

"What's this?" Recoiling slightly, Andrey Andreevich looked at the book as if it were an object he had never seen before.

"It's for you," Yefim said, smiling even more broadly and edging the book toward the director. "It's my book."

"This isn't necessary," the director said. Gingerly, he moved the book away with both hands, as though it might explode. "I have books of my own."

"No, you misunderstood me," Yefim explained, as if to a child. "It isn't just any book, it's my book, I'm the one who wrote it."

"I understand, but it's not necessary," the director said.

"But—but what do you mean?" Yefim stammered. "This isn't a bribe, it's a symbolic gift from the author.

In token of sincere respect and admiration. What's more, I've inscribed it to you, which makes it a unique copy."

"I do not," the director said frostily, "need other people's things, unique or not."

"But this isn't a *thing!*" Yefim said in a voice almost tearful. "It's a book, it has spiritual value. Especially with an author's autograph. Nobody would refuse. I even gave one to a minister—"

"I am not interested in what you gave to whom." The director stood up, leaned across the desk, and shoved the book into Yefim's open attaché case. "Take it away, and don't keep me any longer from my work."

Insulted, injured, spurned, Yefim left the office on unsteady legs.

"Well, how did it go?" Serafima Borisovna asked him.

"Well," Yefim replied with a twisted smile. And he walked out into the street.

It had turned colder. Snow was falling. Yefim walked like a sick old man, limping under the weight of his attaché case that bulged with totally unneeded books about decent people.

"Fima! Fima!" He heard a voice behind him and turned around.

It was Mylnikov, chasing after him with his unbuttoned fur coat, his hat in his hands. You could tell from his face that he bore important news. Yefim suddenly had the foolish, wild, totally absurd idea that perhaps the director of the co-op had asked Mylnikov to overtake him, stop him, bring him back . . .

Absurd, indeed. The director of a co-op, were he from the security system three times over, could not send the world-famous Mylnikov chasing after the little-known writer Rakhlin. But Yefim stopped and froze in anticipation of a miracle.

"Listen," Mylnikov said, fanning himself with his badger hat as he tried to catch his breath. "I completely forgot. Also the . . . the *Yorkshire Post* had an article on me, almost a full page. With my picture . . . They say I'm a present-day Kafka."

In the evening Yefim had guests: two polar researchers and their wives, as well as Tishka and his new girlfriend, whose name was Dasha. Dasha's father worked somewhere abroad as an Aeroflot representative, a fact broadcast by her attire.

The conversation did not go well at first. The polar researchers were reticent; their host's status as a writer made them uncomfortable. The girl was here for the first time and she too was constrained, casting a swift, keen glance now at Yefim, now at Kukusha. The young people did not stay long, however. After dinner they endured another half hour, then ceremoniously took their leave. Tishka called his father out to the hall, cadged five rubles for a taxi, and saw Dasha home. She lived in the neighborhood of River Station.

After their departure, the polar researchers, who by that time were already a little tipsy, gradually loosened up. Interrupting each other and guffawing, they began to recount humorous incidents from their work. The stories were not sophisticated. A man fell through the ice and instead of "Save me!" cried, for some reason, "Watch out below!" Another stole a jar of caviar one night from the kitchen and then was caught when he came down with diarrhea. But their favorite story was about an expedition chief who went out "to do his business" one morning and, as he was crouching behind a snowdrift, felt someone lick his behind. This story, if it ever really happened, had become a legend. The chief, thinking it was the purser, asked, "Is that you, Prokhorov?" When there was no reply, he looked around, saw a polar bear, and ran, losing his pants along the way. The conversation of fearless people usually ended up in the telling of such yarns. Yefim knew them all by heart, but always laughed louder than anyone. But today, with the insult inflicted at the LitFund rankling, he merely tittered politely—falsely, and he knew it.

But after several glasses of Armenian cognac, he too got in the mood. He sat at the piano and accompanied Kukusha, who sang several dirty limericks for the guests. The guests were embarrassed at first, but then it turned out that one of the two wives knew comic love songs from the Vologda region, songs of a raunchiness that far outstripped Kukusha's repertoire. In short, the evening was successful. The guests left after midnight and for a long time continued to shout up from the street, while Yefim stood on the snow-covered balcony, also shouting and waving. Then he sent Kukusha to bed (she had to go to work in the morning), carried the dishes out to the kitchen himself, and slowly washed them, waiting for Tishka's return and deliberating how he would develop the plot of *Operation!* He did not once think about either the hat or Andrey Andreevich.

Tishka came in shortly after two, refused tea, and went to his room. At a quarter to three Yefim crept under the covers with Kukusha, who slept peacefully with her face to the wall. Yefim, lying against her back, felt a surge of desire. Despite his age and high blood pressure, he was still verile and pestered Kukusha more often than she liked. Not wanting to wake his wife too abruptly, he began to stroke her, gradually progressing from the upper erogenous zones to the lower, following a scheme he had learned from the photocopy of an American marriage manual that was circulating in samizdat. (Yefim had discovered the photocopy one day in the bottom drawer of Tishka's desk, had studied it with a dictionary at his side, and had copied the main principles into his notebook, in code.)

Reaching the target of his lust and using a finger as instructed, he succeeded in getting Kukusha to breathe irregularly, though she wasn't awake. When she turned over on her back with a sigh, he immediately took charge of the situation and went to work, his bald head bobbing steadily.

He had lived with Kukusha for about three decades, but he still loved her physically. His former passion was gone, but it had been replaced by a regularly occurring, leisurely, and slowly increasing enjoyment, an enjoyment that began with a general light-headedness and the sensation of sailing away. Now, too, it seemed to Yefim that he was sailing away, that he was Captain Kolomiytsev, feet wide apart, standing on the bridge, an old salt with white temples and a fierce light in his squinting gray eyes. All around were frothy waves, a stormy sea. Ragged, low-flying clouds gathered together, turned into white swans that glided smoothly and slowly overhead, and he rose to meet them, and sailed along with them. . . .

"So what did they tell you about the hat?" Kukusha asked suddenly—loudly, unexpectedly—and it was as if she had shot him out of the sky.

"What?" he asked, and although he didn't stop what he was doing, he lost the rhythm, started fluttering like a bird with a broken wing.

"What," Kukusha repeated sharply, "did they tell you at the co-op?"

It was not, of course, their first conversation of this kind. Kukusha often opened discussions in this position, discussions about such everyday problems as rearranging the furniture, buying a new refrigerator, or obtaining a season ticket to the swimming pool. Yefim always found it unsettling, but now he was particularly unsettled. A dull ache tightened at the back of his head.

"They told me that Mylnikov was written up in the London *Times,* but all I'm getting is fluffy tomcat."

"Fluffy *what?*"

"Tomcat. Ordinary house cat. Even Kostya got rabbit, but I'm getting cat."

He tried to complete what he'd begun, but it was not going well at all.

"So what did you do?"

"I was upset," Yefim said. "I left."

"You left."

"Yes."

"Wonderful!" And Kukusha slid out from under him and turned to the wall.

It was not the first time she had shown her displeasure this way. It always wounded his masculine dignity, and he would plead with her to express her feelings in some other way and let him finish.

This time he did not plead, he turned away himself. He couldn't sleep—his resentment was too great. He got up, went to the kitchen, had a cigarette, and applied an ice pack to his head. They he returned and lay down again with his back to Kukusha.

In the morning he gave Tishka breakfast, drank some coffee himself, and went to his study. He heard Kukusha get up and walk around, slamming the doors and dropping things for his benefit. Finally, she couldn't restrain herself and, already in her fur coat, marched in on him.

"The hat isn't the point. The point is, you're a meliorist who never stands up for himself. You've sunk so low in the eyes of everyone, they won't even give you rabbit!"

Yefim stared dumbly out the window. He could see only the dirty sky, the rime-covered treetops, and the roof of the film workers' cooperative apartment building. Roped to the film workers' chimney, a man was fussing with a television antenna.

"If I were in your shoes, I'd call Karetnikov."

With this advice, Kukusha departed, leaving Yefim in a state of indecision. Perhaps he had been wrong to take a conciliatory position, a posture of compliance and passivity. And, of course, the hat wasn't the point. The point was that he, Rakhlin, was a quiet man. You could always put Rakhlin at the back, at the bottom. Rakhlin would endure it. Rakhlin would say nothing.

"So much for Rakhlin saying nothing!" he cried suddenly, and made an extremely indecent gesture at the stuffed penguin. "No," he went on, "I won't leave it at this. I'll call Karetnikov. I'll go see Karetnikov. All Karetnikov has to do is pick up the phone, and you personally, Andrey Andreevich, even if you did come from the security system—and by the way, why *did* they kick you out?—you personally will bring it to me. Not fluffy tomcat either, or rabbit, but muskrat, you'll bring me muskrat, you personally, in your teeth. *In your teeth!*" he shouted straight in the penguin's face.

And I don't think Yefim overestimated his protector's ability. Vasily Stepanovich Karetnikov was a foremost Soviet writer, a public figure, Hero of Socialist Labor, a deputy to the Supreme Soviet of the USSR, a member of the Communist Party Central Committee, Lenin Prize laureate, State Prize laureate, Gorky Prize laureate, a member of an international committee on the struggle for peace, vice president of the Afro-Asian Friendship Society, a member of the Veterans' Council, a secretary of the Writers' Union, and chief editor of a literary magazine in which Yefim was occasionally published. Karetnikov had indeed made phone calls on Yefim's behalf, or written letters, using his official stationery, and his calls and his letters always did their work.

Karetnikov, however, happened to be away. His wife, Larisa Yevgenevna, said that he was traveling in Africa. After Africa, he would be in Paris for a meeting of some UNESCO commission. He would be back in about three weeks.

But if Yefim waited three weeks, the orders would all

be taken, and even the rabbit fur would be all cut. No, Yefim had made up his mind; he could think of nothing now but the hat. He decided to go see Lukin.

The Moscow branch of the Writers' Union, together with the Central Literary Club, occupies two connecting buildings and has two entrances—one from Vorovskoy Street, and the other, the main entrance, from Herzen Street. At both entrances are great double doors of carved oak and thick glass. The offices of the bosses are located here, as well as lecture halls for speeches, concerts, and film showings. There is also a restaurant, a billiards room, a barber shop, and all sorts of other amenities for the writers.

In the spacious lobby of the main entrance Yefim was met by the two perpetual attendants, Rozalia Moiseevna and Yekaterina Ivanovna.

He came here often. Occasionally—and on Women's Day, always—he presented the lobby ladies with perfume, chocolate, and his novels. So they both greeted him very cordially.

"Hello, Yefim Semyonovich!"

"Yefim Semyonovich! You haven't been in for quite a while."

"Yes, quite a while, quite a while," echoed the cloakroom attendant, Vladimir Ilyich, taking Yefim's sheepskin.

Receiving his ticket from the cloakroom attendant, Yefim saw two familiar figures sitting at a chess table in the far corner: his downstairs neighbor Vaska Tryoshkin and a secretary of the Writers' Union, Victor Cherpakov. They were not playing chess; heads close together, they were discussing something in tense whispers. Seeing Yefim, they returned his nod reluctantly.

Yefim put his ticket in the side pocket of his jacket, picked up his attaché case, and headed for the stairs leading to the second floor.

"There," Tryoshkin said, following Yefim with a long, heavy stare. "My tomcat disappears, and they give him a hat made of tomcat fur. How am I to interpret that?"

"If we sit here long enough, doing nothing, they'll make hats out of us, too," Cherpakov said.

This was the continuation of a topic they had begun back in the restaurant and now resumed here in the corner.

Not only did Cherpakov not dispel Tryoshkin's fears about Hebraization, but he asserted that Tryoshkin was underestimating rather than exaggerating the extent of the international Jewish conspiracy. According to Cherpakov, the Jews had taken over not only America and the other countries of the West, but they were virtually running the General Staff, the KGB, and even the Politburo.

"The Politburo? That's going a little far," Tryoshkin said doubtfully. "There are no Zionists there."

"Zionists, no. Freemasons, yes. And the Freemasons are controlled by the Zionists."

"What salvation is there?" Tryoshkin asked in horror.

"None," Cherpakov replied. "Unless we exterminate them, one by one."

"You'd never exterminate them all," Tryoshkin sighed.

"Not all, perhaps. But at least a few."

"Fima, now tell the truth. You were never unfaithful to your Kukusha, not even once?"

They were sitting in a narrow corridor in front of Lukin's dark-green Leatherette-covered door. Yefim was here on his hat business, and the poetess Natalya Knysh was hoping to receive a character reference for a trip to Portugal. Natalya was a small, soft, sexy lady. In a voice husky from smoking, she said: "You know what Chekhov said about Korolenko? He said that Korolenko was too virtuous a man to be a good writer. That Korolenko would write a lot better if he was unfaithful to his wife, at least once."

Yefim smiled politely, but didn't feel like flirting. He was wondering what the best approach would be to take with Lukin.

Pyotr Nikolaevich Lukin, as was indicated on the nameplate, silver letters on black, was the union's Moscow Division Secretary for Organizational Matters, and he belonged to a breed of men which, thank God, has today practically become extinct in our country. Like Andrey Andreevich, like many another, he came to the Writers' Union from the security system, where he had traveled the route from prison guard to general. The System was his family, home, school, religion, and philosophy. All of his life and all of his health he had given to the System. He had served the System, had imprisoned in its name, had been imprisoned in its name, and was rehabilitated in its name. For his loyalty and unswerving justice he received the Friendship of the Peoples medal, the chest insignia of Distinguished Chekist, and the title Honored Servant of Fine Arts, which the wits, of course, had abbreviated to the acronym HORSEFART.

Although he served in another department now, he knew that he belonged, in every fiber of his being, body and soul, only to the security system. To the Party, too, of course. But the Party and the System, for him, were one.

He had a special kind of memory, or, rather, two separate memories in the same head: a police memory that applied to present cases, and a general-historical memory for grasping the overall course of his life. In his youth Lukin had been a romantic, and indeed he remained one, since his general-historical memory was romantic, preserving only a pleasantly misty picture of uninterrupted, selfless service. Such details as the fact that he himself, personally, had knocked out someone's teeth for the sake of the triumph of a high ideal, or even that his own teeth had been knocked out for the same ideal, receded into the shadows, dissolved into the muddy blur of the past. Who had knocked out whose teeth did not matter. What mattered was that throughout these vicissitudes he had not once, not even for a minute, doubted the System, doubted the rightness of Our Common Cause. Now, suffering from insomnia, he looked back on his life, the ordeals, the humiliations, and with tears of tender pride reflected that he had never, not once . . .

And the Party appreciated his devotion. And the System still looked after him; it had got him this job with the writers. As he labored here in a situation so unlike his previous duties, so complex, he came to look upon this assignment as a mission behind enemy lines.

Tall, skinny, nearsighted, he had a horsey face and a smile that made him resemble the French actor Fernandel. The smile never left his face, because the System, providing him with his government teeth, had made them a little too long and wide. His hair was light with a reddish cast; thinning, but only slightly, and streaked, but not much, with gray.

His duties consisted of drafting and processing government forms. In these forms he always adhered to the truth, but sometimes distorted it beyond all recognition. He could construe any statement or act or gesture as an attempt to undermine the foundations of our regime, and could build up such a damning case that one felt that all that remained was to pass sentence. Or he could use the exact same facts to recommend someone for a medal or to register him in a housing cooperative. The writers appreciated Lukin because despite his skill with forms, he did not try to be a writer himself. But he could have been, because in the genre of forms he knew no equal, in fact the man was practically a genius.

As he waited in front of Lukin's dark-green door, Yefim did not know that on the other side of that door he was already being scrutinized. A thick file for the letter *R* had been removed from an iron safe. From the file a slim folder with the number 14/6 had been pulled. In that folder were only a few pages, but each page was worth its weight in gold. Lukin could have asked for any writer's dossier from the Creative Personnel Department, but he didn't need to; he had his own notes, short and businesslike, based on data gathered by his own informers.

Always, before receiving a person, Lukin glanced at his notes. He was doing this now. Here is what he read:

"Rakhlin Yefim Semyonovich (Shmulevich) 7/13/27, w. Kukushkina Zin. Ivan. (dnn. Kukusha), s. Timofey gs., d. Natalya Is., fr. No. 2/14., J., wv., 5med./11bk./2fs./1p., WHNLV, dim./ninvwo./nkvi., mdhicp(p)., LER, mcbwttdrelinc."

But let us decode these abbreviations:

w.—wife
dnn.—domestic nickname
s.—son
gs.—graduate student
d.—daughter
Is.—Israel
fr.—friend
No. 2/14—Kostya Baranov was listed in the file under this number
J.—Jew
wv.—war veteran
5med./11bk./2fs./1p.—5 medals, 11 books, 2 film scripts, 1 play
WHNLV—work has no literary value
dim./ninvwo./nkvi.—drinks in moderation, not involved with women, no known vices
mdhicp(p).—modest, discreet, harmless, interested in chess and politics (passively)
LER—listens to enemy radio
mcbwttdrelinc.—might collaborate, but with ten-

dency to deviation, reliable inside the country (that is, he shouldn't be let out)

Assessing these data in accordance with the measuring stick of human qualities used by Lukin, we might get something like this:

w.—positive factor; in an emergency the w. can be used as leverage
dnn.—bespeaks decency and a stable family life
s. and d.—additional safeguards; see w.
gs.—even better
Is.—potential unreliability
fr.—possible informer
J.—see Is.
wv.—good
5med./11bk./2fs./1p.—relative prosperity, hence little dissatisfaction and inclination to antisocial acts
WHNLV—in combination with the previous point, a positive factor; ambitions will be modest
dim./ninvwo./nkvi.—a negative combination; provides little leverage
mdhicp(p).—no problem; provided (p)
LER—good; can be used in place of knvi.
mcbwttdrelinc.—not the best recruiting material

Pyotr Nikolaevich Lukin liked to know why his visitors came, and he almost always did know. He knew this time, too. He had a communication from the director of the LitFund co-op, and in addition something had been reported to him by Rakhlin's neighbor Fishkin, the fairy-tale writer.

To Pyotr Nikolaevich's specialized skills one must add the fact that he was a great expert on human weakness and a talented liar. Before inviting Yefim in, he took his expensive coat with the reindeer-fawn collar and his reindeer-fawn hat from the rack and put them in the storeroom adjoining his office. From the storeroom he brought out and hung on the rack a raincoat with a quilted lining and a navy-blue beret.

This done, he peered out into the corridor. Seeing Yefim, he feigned unfeigned surprise.

"Ah, Yefim Semyonovich!" he cried, as if delighted. "You wanted to see me? But why are you sitting there? You should have knocked right away! Well, come in, do come in. Wait, wait, mustn't shake hands across the threshold!"

And, drawing Yefim into the office, he embraced him heartily, even slapped him on the back, and peppered him with personal questions, from which one could tell that he thought of Yefim often. "Well, how's your health? How are things? How's Kukusha? Everything's all right with Tishka at graduate school? My grandson's a graduate student, too, as it happens. At the film institute. A remarkable lad. Athlete, mountain climber, Komsomol leader. They say there are no young people these days devoted to ideals. But I look at Petya—he's named after me, you know—and I see we do have good young people, top-notch young people. Oh, of course there are deviations as well." The general took off his glasses and wiped them with his handkerchief. "Speaking of that, how's Natasha? A sore subject, I realize. I don't ask officially, you understand, not from the—ha-ha—intelligence point of view, but as a father myself and even as a grandfather . . . She's settled somehow, I hope? Not short of money? Everything's all right with her family?"

He knew, of course, that Yefim went every Tuesday to the main post office, pulling his hat down over his eyes and covering his face. It is unclear what Yefim hoped to achieve by this because there he extended through the little window a passport with a photograph in which his prominent Jewish eyes and face were completely unconcealed. But Yefim, not knowing that Lukin knew, reported, with some hesitation, that actually he didn't have much news about his daughter, that he didn't keep in touch with her.

"Oh, but you should," Lukin said. "These aren't the old days, you know, when the presence of relatives abroad could lead to trouble. When that unfortunate incident of mine happened, it turned out that I had an aunt in Argentina. I'd completely forgotten she existed. But they made a note in my file, said that I'd concealed it. Now, thank goodness, that attitude has changed. Today people understand that our children, no matter how they behave, are our children: we still worry about them, work to get them into institutes and graduate schools, buy them shoes, jeans, gloves, hats . . . But forgive me," he said, "you didn't come to see me without a reason. You must have some business matter to discuss."

Yefim was confused, taken aback. It struck him as very strange that Pyotr Nikolaevich himself had broached the subject of hats. After wavering a moment, he nevertheless said that a hat was exactly what he had come to talk about.

“A hat?” Pyotr Nikolaevich raised his light eyebrows in surprise.

“A hat,” Yefim said, nodding, and straightaway launched into a tangled, stumbling explanation of how he had gone to the co-op and how the man in charge there—of course Yefim had the greatest respect for him—no doubt he man had been a valued colleague in the security system—but, after all, as everyone knew, it took a certain special tact and a sensitivity to work with people who labored creatively—but he—

“He refused?” With a dark frown Pyotr Nikolaevich reached for the telephone.

“Wait,” Yefim said, stopping him, and began to explain, even more awkwardly, that the man hadn’t refused him exactly, no, but he’d been callous, he hadn’t understood, offering cat to Yefim, the author of eleven books, when even Kostya Baranov, who wrote just one book in his entire life—even Kostya had got rabbit.

While Yefim talked, Pyotr Nikolaevich glanced at his watch and pressed a secret button, with the result that his secretary appeared and reminded him about the meeting he had to attend at the Moscow Soviet.

The conversation took an uncomfortable turn. Pyotr Nikolaevich said that he personally knew nothing about fur hats, and fixed his eyes in abstraction at a point past Yefim, toward the door. Involuntarily looking in the same direction, Yefim saw hanging on the rack the raincoat and the blue beret. This disconcerted him. How could he petition for a fine fur hat when such a good man—and a general—was going around in a beret? Pyotr Nikolaevich, not letting Yefim gather his wits, immediately recounted an episode from his military past. How he and his detachment once broke out of an encirclement and wandered across the snow-covered Salsk steppes, with all the men in ragged summer uniforms, worn shoes, and cotton forage caps. Although Yefim in his own life had more than once known such hardships, he could not help feeling embarrassed that at the present moment he wasn't wandering the snow-covered steppes. That nowadays he spent his nights not under a frozen haystack but in a warm apartment. And that although he had come here without a hat, he did after all own one.

He was ready to surrender, but just then the poet and songwriter Samarin dropped by, fox-fur hat in hand. Samarin fulfilled the duties of Party secretary.

Nodding coolly to Yefim, he asked Pyotr Nikolaevich whether he was going to dinner.

"No," the general said, glancing at his watch. "I'm due at the Moscow Soviet."

"Well, so long," Samarin said. As he left, he waved his hat, making the papers on Pyotr Nikolaevich's desk flutter.

The sight of that hat was a goad to Yefim's fighting spirit, because Samarin may have been a Party organizer but he was worthless as a poet. By no stretch of the imagination did the man rate a fox-fur hat.

Emboldened, Yefim reminded Pyotr Nikolaevich that he too had been in the war. He had participated, moreover, in various dangerous expeditions. But now it was a time of peace, when people had greater aspirations and wanted to satisfy them fully and in fairness. But what fairness could there be, if someone who was chummy with the higher-ups received reindeer fawn, while a man who quietly and self-effacingly toiled to create books about people in fearless professions was given only fluffy tomcat?

"Where," Yefim went on, "where, then, is our much-proclaimed equality? The equality that the newspapers throughout our land write about?"

"Really!" Pyotr Nikolaevich jumped up indignantly. "Yefim, you go too far! Making generalizations like that, and all because of some . . . some fur hat! What does this have to do with equality, what does this have to do with high ideals? Surely you're not suggesting we should sell our ideals for a lousy hat? I don't know, Yefim . . . You're younger than I am. You're another generation. But people of my generation . . . And I personally . . . You know, a lot has happened to me. But I never, never doubted the main thing. Never doubted it, not for one minute."

Pyotr Nikolaevich had turned white as a sheet and started to tremble. With shaking hands he reached into a side pocket, pulled out his wallet, and took from it a small yellowed photograph.

"Here!" he said, and threw his last trump on the desk in front of Yefim.

Yefim picked up the photograph and saw the image of a little girl, six or eight years old, with a big white bow in her hair.

"My daughter," the general whispered with emotion. "That's how she looked when they took me. And I left—" He shrugged and smiled bitterly. "I left without any hat at all. . . . And when I returned, she . . . my daughter was already a big girl. Married . . ."

He brushed a tear from his cheek and waved his hand. Mumbling, "Excuse me, it's time for me to go," he carefully put the photograph back in his wallet and the wallet back in his pocket, then got into his raincoat and put on his blue beret.

Yefim was filled with shame. He felt like a loathsome, scheming insect. He felt, even, that somehow it was his own mercenary complaints that had caused Pyotr Nikolaevich, years ago, to be snatched from his little daughter and led away hatless into the dark.

Muttering an apology, head bowed, Yefim shuffled to the exit.

Only downstairs did he realize how late it was—the Central Literary Club was beginning its evening life; the billiards room and restaurant had opened. In the lecture hall upstairs a television crew was setting up their equipment to cover a meeting between writers and cosmonauts; in the smaller downstairs hall the members of the Storytellers' Club were gathering; and in the famous Room 8 a personal case was being heard, that of the prose writer Nikitin, who had allowed a foreign publisher to publish his short novel *From the Life of a Worm,* which libelously depicted the Soviet people as worms. Nikitin himself swore that by worms he meant worms only, nothing more or less, and it was actually the truth, but of course no one believed him.

The glass doors banged constantly. Rozalia Moiseevna and Yekaterina Ivanovna were dissolving in smiles before the entering bosses, greeting the people they knew, and requiring those they didn't to present membership cards or invitations.

By the cloakroom, as he pulled on his sheepskin, Yefim encountered Kostya Baranov coming in from the cold. He wore a dark coat and a brown rabbit-fur hat.

"Yefim!" Kostya said, glad to see his friend. "Look, I got my hat already. What's more, I snagged a hundred rubles for a couple of in-house reviews. Let's go to the restaurant. My treat."

"Not in the mood," Yefim said, picking up his attaché case. "Nothing to celebrate, either. I made nothing today, and the hat they're giving me is tomcat, fluffy tomcat."

Kostya blinked. "Tomcat?"

"Ordinary house cat," Yefim explained. "You wrote one book, they give you rabbit. I wrote eleven and get cat."

Vaska Tryoshkin overheard this exchange as he put on his coat in front of the mirror, but learned nothing new.

"Fima," Kostya said, "why take it out on me? I'm not in the business of distributing hats. As far as I'm concerned, they can give you sable."

Yefim did not reply; he was staring open-mouthed at Pyotr Nikolaevich Lukin running past toward the exit, at Lukin's reindeer fawn collar, at Lukin's reindeer fawn hat.

For a moment Yefim was thunderstruck. Then he darted out after Lukin, wanting to stop him. But he was too late: the Volga, with the general inside, pulled away from the curb, spitting malodorous smoke. Yefim watched it go, his eyes desperate.

He shifted his attaché case from his left hand to his right and trudged off toward Insurrection Square. He trudged like an old man, scuffing the soles of his East

German boots and muttering and sobbing under his breath. "Lies! All lies! The Salsk steppes, your daughter—all lies! You left and she was eight, you came back six years later and she was married. Stupid!" he shouted into the air. "Stupid!"

Preoccupied with his pain, Yefim did not see that he was being followed. Behind him, not letting him out of sight, was the poet Vaska Tryoshkin, who had decided to study and understand the mysterious behavior of Zionists.

At Sadovaya Circle all the traffic lights were blinking yellow; traffic was being directed by two policemen who wore dark sheepskin coats and hats with turned-down earflaps. Both men, for some reason, were short-tempered. They stopped crowds of pedestrians on the sidewalk, blew their whistles, brandished their sticks. Not realizing what was happening, Yefim pushed ahead, but they allowed him no farther, so he stood under one of the blinkers, and there his bald pate blinked, too, with a venomous yellow light.

In the crowd huddling around the traffic signal Vaska lost sight of Yefim. Or perhaps—he wouldn't have been surprised—the Zionist had simply dissolved into thin air. Nervous, Vaska elbowed his way through the crowd, and froze. He saw the Zionist Rakhlin standing at the edge of the sidewalk muttering incantations while his bald pate pulsed yellow signals into outer space.

"Citizens, refrain from crossing!" boomed voices from another world. The policeman standing not far from Yefim leaped out of the road, drew himself up, and raised a stiff hand to his temple. Then black silhouettes bore down on them and swooped past them with wailing sirens, snorting motors, swishing tires, and flashing, blinking lights.

Vaska Tryoshkin was transfixed. He stared at the head of Zionist Rakhlin. Before, it had blinked yellow; now it flared blue and red.

This, of course, was the ideal moment to seize the Zionist and deliver him into the hands of the law. But the law itself—the government limousines driving past—was transmitting the same treacherous signals! Suddenly Vaska was frightened. He clutched his head, his eyes shut tight. When he opened them, he found himself sitting on the ice-covered sidewalk, his back against a rough wall. A crowd had gathered around him, and the policeman who bent over him was inquiring kindly, "Pop! Hey, pop! Are you drunk or sick, or what?"

Standing under the traffic light, Yefim heard voices discussing whether to call an ambulance or have the individual taken to the drunk tank. Normally he would have gone over to see what had happened; he was always curious about street dramas. But this time he did not look. Immersed in his own trouble, he trudged on as soon as the way was clear. At the Krasnaya Presnya metro the stream of humanity caught Yefim, pulled him underground, and ejected him, badly rumpled, at Airport Station.

Meanwhile, Vaska was proceeding to the same terminal by a completely different route. Left alone by the policeman and the crowd, he did not walk toward Presnya but headed for Mayakovsky Street.

It was a cold, clear evening, but the city lights made the sky a bilious yellow. Nevertheless, stars broke through, twinkled, winked, hinting at something Vaska could not fathom. Cars rolled along, people hurried past, but who among them were Jews and Yid-Masons, no one knew. He kept on walking, deep in thought, and suddenly at the corner of Bolshaya Bronnaya and Sadovo-Kudrinskaya streets he was struck by a brilliant idea. If they had already taken over everything, maybe Vaska would be better off giving in to them, joining them—now, before it was too late.

At home, Yefim set his attaché case in the corner, changed from boots to slippers, and went to the living room. Kukusha and Tishka were eating supper in front of the television, watching the figure skating.

Yefim sat down on the couch to watch too, but he saw nothing, heard nothing.

"Baldy," Kukusha asked, "are you going to eat supper?"

He did not answer.

"Baldy!" Kukusha said, raising her voice.

He did not hear.

"Baldy!" she shouted. "I'm asking you, do you want butter or sour cream on your dumplings?"

"Eighteen," Yefim replied.

"Eighteen what?"

"Eighteen years in the Writers' Union, and eleven

books," Yefim said. And added, after a moment's thought, "Kostya wrote only one."

Mother and son exchanged looks.

"Baldy," Kukusha said, nervous. "You haven't gone and lost your marbles, have you?"

"No," Yefim said, "I won't leave it at this. I'll get that hat. If it kills me."

Suddenly he jumped up, ran to the hall, and returned with his wolf-fur hat.

"Tishka, you like my hat?"

"Sure." Tishka swallowed his last dumpling and wiped his lips with a paper napkin.

"Then here," Yefim said. "I make you a present of it." He jammed the hat on Tishka's head. "It looks good on you."

"And you'll wear mine?" Tishka asked. He took off the hat, inspected it, set it on the chair beside him.

"Yours?" Yefim said. "Yours you can throw away. It's worn."

"But what will you wear?"

"I'm getting a hat," Yefim said. "If it kills me."

"Baldy, have something to eat." Kukusha laid a plate of dumplings on the table. "Sit, eat, forget about the goddamn hat. This is all my fault. I put you up to it. Look, to hell with the hat. I'll buy you one myself, a better one than any of your asshole writers have. I'll buy you . . . how about silver fox?"

"No!" Yefim shouted. "Absolutely not! I'll make them! When Karetnikov comes back, I'll go see him and then . . ."

He shook his fist and started to weep.

I first heard about Yefim going mad from Baranov, on the phone, and then from Fishkin at the Literary Club. I put off calling Yefim, and then one morning, well before nine, Kukusha appeared at my door in a mink coat that glistened with melted snowflakes.

"Excuse me for not calling first," Kukusha began. "But I didn't want anyone to know I was coming here."

"Never mind," I said, "it doesn't matter. Excuse my being in pajamas."

"It's quite all right. Nice pajamas, by the way. Where did you get them?"

"My sister brought them from France."

"You have a sister in France?" Kukusha was surprised.

"No, my sister's in Izhevsk. But she went to France to negotiate something with the Renault people. Coffee?"

"No, no, I'm only staying a minute." And, in a completely different tone: "I need your help. You must save Yefim."

I asked what the trouble was, what he needed saving from.

Kukusha said: "He doesn't eat, he doesn't drink, he doesn't sleep, shave, or brush his teeth. He always used to make fried eggs for Tishka in the morning. Now the boy leaves for the institute without his breakfast."

"The boy's twenty-four. I would think he could fry his own eggs."

"Forget about the eggs," Kukusha said impatiently. "It's Fima. He's completely fixated on this hat. He's been to see all the big shots—at the LitFund, the Writers' Union—and they've turned him down everywhere. Now he goes around all the time saying, 'Eighteen years in the Writers' Union, eleven books, and I was decorated.' I say to him, 'Baldy, what's happening to you? Fuck the goddamn hat!' His answer is that he'll get the hat if it kills him, and he's still waiting for his precious Karetnikov. 'Karetnikov will come back,' he says, 'and then we'll see!' But that lousy Karetnikov is in Mongolia, or Portugal, and God knows when he'll be back!" She started to sniffle and reached in her pocket for a handkerchief. "And it's my fault, you know. I pushed him into it, I wanted him to fight, and now I can't stop him. I plead with him, 'Baldy, darling, please, I'll buy you ten hats.' But all he says is 'Eighteen years, eleven books, and I was decorated.' "

"Perhaps . . . a psychiatrist?"

Kukusha sighed. "Perhaps. But it might be better, after all, to wait for Karetnikov. If he helped . . . In the meantime, if you could just see Fima, amuse him somehow. Have a friendly talk. Ask him what he's writing, when he'll finish it. That kind of thing always has a good effect on him."

I visited Yefim and found him, indeed, a changed man. Gaunt and disheveled, he received me in a wrinkled sweat suit with a hole in one knee. His face was covered with a salt-and-pepper stubble.

"Hello, Yefim!" I said.

"Hello."

Blocking the doorway, he looked at me with an expression of neither pleasure nor displeasure.

"You might let me in," I said.

He followed me in.

"May I sit down?" I asked.

He shrugged. "Sit."

I sat in the armchair in the corner under the antlers. He stood in front of me.

"I'm seeing my eye doctor," I said, "and decided to drop in while I was at it."

He nodded, chewing at the black nail on his little finger, but didn't appear to be listening. I told him all sorts of interesting things. The awful behavior of the children's writer Filenkin, for example. At a writers' lodge, Filenkin had thrown his soup into the director's face. Yefim smiled politely. Finishing with the pinkie, he went to work on his ring finger. The latest racial incidents in South Africa and the reshuffling of Margaret Thatcher's cabinet also failed to spark his interest.

I suggested a game of chess. He nodded, but when he set up the pieces, he put the king and queen in the wrong position. He lost right in the opening, even though he was a much stronger player than I.

We began a new game, and I asked him how *Operation!* was going.

"Eighteen years a member of the Writers' Union and eleven books," he replied, moving his queen to a square where it could be taken.

At this point the telephone rang. As Yefim turned to answer it, I moved his queen to a safer square.

"What?" Yefim shouted suddenly. "Back? When? Good. Thanks. Take care. We'll talk tonight."

He slammed down the receiver and faced me. I beheld the former Yefim, albeit unshaven.

"You heard," he told me, extremely excited. "That was Kostya. He says Karetnikov's back."

It's difficult to describe what happened next. Yefim kept jumping up, running around the room and waving his arms, and muttering something to the effect that now he would give that so-and-so what for. Then he returned to the chessboard, mated me in four moves, looked at his watch, and said it was probably time for me to go to my doctor.

I left, rejoicing to see Yefim so quickly recovered, though the credit for his recovery was not mine.

The events that followed I relate partly from Yefim's own account and partly from the accounts—contradictory—of the other participants in the story.

As soon as I left, Yefim washed and shaved, then brushed his false teeth and put them in. Between these operations he kept dialing Karetnikov, and finally got through. Karetnikov's wife, Larisa Yevgenevna, said that Vasily Stepanovich was under the weather and not receiving anyone, but the voice of the alleged invalid came on the line.

"Fima!" he roared. "Don't listen to her. Grab a taxi and be here in five minutes. And bring your manuscript!"

Karetnikov lived in a high-rise on Insurrection Square.

When Larisa Yevgenevna opened the door to Yefim, she was wearing a bathrobe, had curlers in her hair, and her face was covered with cream.

"Well, come in, now that you're here," she said, none

too cordially. "Vasily Stepanovich is waiting. In his tuxedo."

Yefim walked down a long hall past the maid, Nadya, who was standing on a rickety stepladder and brushing a cobweb off the ceiling with a mop. She wore a very short chintz housecoat.

"Hello, Nadya," Yefim said, but then quickly looked down, averting his eyes.

The door of Karetnikov's study opened, and Yefim's host revealed himself in gym shorts and a T-shirt that had burn holes over his great belly. He pulled Yefim inside and shut the door.

"Did you bring it?" he asked in an urgent whisper.

"I did," Yefim said, and drew from his attaché case not a manuscript but a split of vodka.

"Is that all?"

Yefim smiled. "There's a second volume, too." He opened the attaché case slightly and showed him: a second split lay at the bottom.

"Good job!" Karetnikov said approvingly. He pulled the cork with his teeth and like a juggler twirled the bottle, making the vodka froth up in a spiral and shoot into his greedily open mouth.

After finishing about a third of it in this manner, the host gasped, grunted, and hid the bottle behind a book on the bookshelf, Marx's *Das Kapital.*

"Good job!" he repeated, panting. "That's what I call Jewish smarts. Why am I opposed to anti-Semitism? Because the Jew, in moderation, is a necessary element in our society. At my office, for example, I'm Russian, my deputy's Russian—that's as it should be. But for my executive secretary I always take a Jew. My last secretary was a Jew, and so's the one I have now. When the Central Committee tried to palm off Novikov on me in place of Rubinstein, I told them: Not on your life! If you want me to continue to put out a genuine, Party-minded literary journal, comrades, don't you touch my Jews. I've been an editor thirty-six years now—I lived through it all—but even in the days of cosmopolitanism hunting I always had Jews. And they always knew I wouldn't let them get hurt. But I demand that they in turn be loyal. I called Leykin into the office, treated him to a glass of vodka. Well, Nyomka, I said, if you're eyeing your historic homeland, be a good boy and clear out of here first, and fast, at least six months before you apply. Otherwise I'll rip off your legs, put matchsticks in their place, and make you walk to Israel."

His meat hands folded behind his back, his belly protruding, Karetnikov paced the room and talked on and on. Sometimes, when a phrase especially pleased him, he would slap his huge thighs and squeal with laughter. Then he turned and asked if Yefim had seen his article.

"Where?" Yefim asked quickly.

"My dear friend, you mean you don't read *Pravda*? Tsk-tsk. Ah, you see how I caught you? Don't worry, don't worry, I won't give you away. Here." He grabbed the newspaper from his desk and thrust it at Yefim. " 'Always with the Party, Always with the People.' Nice headline, eh?"

"Mmm . . ." Yefim began hesitantly.

"Mmooo!" Karetnikov lowed, mimicking. "Don't squirm, don't mumble. I can see you're turning up your nose. The title's no gem. It's simple, though, straightforward. Always with the Party, always with the people.

Always with them both. Not like those . . ." He did not finish. Groaning, he ran to the door, clutched his ears, and with them banged his head three times—as if it were an inanimate object—against the door frame. "I despise you!" he snarled through clenched teeth. "Despise, despise, despise you!" He glowered at Yefim. "You know whom I despise, don't you? You know, but you're afraid to say. Our beloved regime, our Soviet State . . . I des-pise you!" Again he banged his head against the wall.

Then he began to pace around Yefim, muttering half to himself.

"There it is, human ingratitude. The state gave me everything, and I despise it. Without it, what would I be? Nothing. With it, what am I? A writer! Writer deputy, writer laureate, writer hero, foremost writer Vaska Karetnikov!" He stopped and faced Yefim. "But Vaska Karetnikov should have been in business, like his Grandpa Tikhon. Tikhon Karetnikov, leather goods and hardware. Owned two steamships on the Volga. My daddy, Stepan Tikhonovich, got the firing squad for those steamships. In the orphanage I changed my origin to 'peasant.' And began to write a little in the newspaper *The Blacksmith* under the pseudonym Been Around. I sent Gorky a short story, 'Time of Breakthrough,' and he was fool enough to print it in his almanac. Bastards! You destroyed Vaska Karetnikov, you made a writer out of him. I hate you!" He went to bang his head once more against the door frame, but instead touched his head and winced.

"Vasily Stepanovich!" Yefim whispered, pointing at the ceiling.

Karetnikov understood. "Microphones there, you think?" he said. "Well, of course there are. But I don't give a shit. Because what I say here doesn't matter. Everyone knows: Karetnikov drinks, what can you expect of him? It only matters what I say in public. Here, I say what I want. Especially now that they've insulted me, the sons of bitches. They promised to make me academician, but instead they gave it to Shushugin. Academician Shushugin. And the academician says 'liberry' instead of 'library'—and that's the truth! Shushugin they made an academician, me they insulted, and everyone knows it, so I can shoot my mouth off. But only at home, because the Party demands our devotion, not our hearts. I am allowed to despise it, but when required, I am the Party's soldier. You're a writer, you're supposed to understand the difference between the words *allowed* and *required*. I do what is required, and therefore I am allowed much. If you don't do what is required, you are allowed less. Much less. That's dialectics. Another swallow!"

Karetnikov sat in a leather chair and shut his eyes. By the time Yefim fetched the bottle from behind Karl Marx and returned to Karetnikov, his host was snoring.

Yefim sat down opposite him, holding the bottle in his hands. Time passed. A clock in a wooden case struck half past eleven. Yefim looked around him, studying the room. A desk and chair of antique workmanship. Modern bookshelves, crammed with the works of Marx, Engels, Lenin, and the General Secretary. The General Secretary most prominently. At one time, volumes of Stalin had been displayed here. Then of Khrushchev.

Then Khrushchev disappeared, and Stalin reappeared. Now in Stalin's place stood a four-volume set of Gustav Husák. So, thought Yefim, the wind is changing again.

At last Karetnikov opened one eye and trained it on Yefim. He opened the other eye and asked, "What time is it?"

"Quarter past one," Yefim whispered, as if still afraid of waking him.

Karetnikov put out his hand. "Give me!"

He took a swig from the bottle, but without his earlier greed, then puckered up his face and shook his head.

"Well, tell me why you're here. What is it you want: a dacha, a car, a vacation in Pitsunda, a subscription to *America*?"

"Oh, no." Yefim smiled, and his smile indicated that his request was far more modest, practically a trifle, that he was embarrassed, really, to trouble such an important man about such a little thing.

"Out with it, out with it," Karetnikov said encouragingly.

Yefim plucked up his nerve and spoke, stating the case as clearly as he could. Karetnikov listened with attention, then took another swig from the bottle and looked at Yefim in a new way.

"So," he said in a voice suddenly sober. "You're not asking for a dacha or a car, you're not planning to go to a writers' lodge, and you don't need *America*. A fur hat, that's all you want. But it can't be just any fur. Cat won't do. Right? Or rabbit, either?"

Yefim smiled and modestly lowered his eyes.

"Only a hat," Karetnikov went on benevolently. "But cat's no good, and rabbit won't do. Would you like, perhaps, a boyar's hat? Sable, perhaps? Who do you think you are!" he suddenly shouted, jumping up and slapping his thighs. "Which one of us is the fool here? Perhaps you think you're a *Yiddishe* genius and I'm a poor dumb Russian fuck who drinks cabbage soup from a bark sandal. You pretending that a dacha's a lot to ask, but a hat is nothing!" he bellowed.

"But Vasily Stepanovich," stammered Yefim, recoiling, "why are you . . . How can you . . . I don't understand."

"Liar!" Karetnikov sneered. "You know as well as I do that you don't need a hat. That you can buy any hat you like for a hundred or two, off some fence. No, it's not a hat you're after. You want to worm your way into a better category, a higher class. You want to be given the same kind of hat that I have, to be treated as an equal with me, with me, who am a secretary of the Writers' Union, a member of the Central Committee, a deputy to the Supreme Soviet, Lenin Prize laureate, vice president of the World Peace Council. That's what you want, isn't it?" Karetnikov patted himself with satisfaction. "Yes. Very clever. Too clever. You'll go on writing about decent people, pretending there's no such thing as the Soviet state, no such thing as district committees and regional committees. And this, wearing the same hat that I wear? Not on your life, my friend. If you really want to be treated equally, as one of us, then you must accept equality in the other things. You must write boldly, as I do, without turning up your nose: 'Always with the Party, Always with the People.' And sit in presidiums for ten, twenty, thirty years wearing a solemn sourpuss face. And deliver a few hundred bureaucratic speeches. *Then* come for your hat. Otherwise—you have to be joking! A better hat for you? On what grounds?

"And I suppose you're envious that I travel abroad and bring back all sorts of clothes. But that's just one side of my life. What you don't see, behind the clothes, is that I'm also out there struggling for peace, for peace in this whole goddamn world. Now, you were in Paris, too, on a tour. Did they ask you questions there? They did. And what did you say? You said you weren't interested in politics. You weren't interested in geography. You weren't even sure where Afghanistan was. But I can't give them a runaround like that. I can't say I'm not interested in politics. I'm required to give a straight answer—and I do. What do I think about Afghanistan? I think those rebels have to be crushed. What do I think about political prisoners? There are political prisoners in South Africa, Chile, and Haiti, I say, but in Soviet jails we have only criminals and madmen. You think it's pleasant for me to say this? It's not pleasant. I too want to smile and be smiled upon. I too want to write about decent people. I too want to ignore politics and geography.

"You think if you don't write against the Soviet regime, we'll say thank you? You're wrong. It's not enough not to be against us. You have to be for us. When you struggle for peace in your writing, as I do, and include secretaries of regional and district committees, then you'll get everything. We'll forgive you for being a Jew, we'll give you a dacha, we'll give you a hat. Reindeer fawn, or muskrat at least. But to anyone who turns up his nose, to anyone who dodges and makes excuses, I say this!" And he gave Yefim the finger.

He made the gesture without thinking, with no idea that it could have dire consequences. And in other circumstances there would have been no dire consequences. But now . . . Even Yefim did not know how the thing happened. When he saw the finger before him, an inch from his nose, he snapped at it like a dog. He bit it hard, to the bone.

The bite was so unexpected that Karetnikov didn't feel the pain immediately. He pulled his hand back, looked at Yefim, looked at his finger, then let out a howl, and staggered crazily around the study, waving his hand and spattering blood on the Persian rug.

Larisa Yevgenevna came running, in her curlers. The maid Nadya appeared, rag in hand.

"What happened, Vasya?" Larisa Yevgenevna screeched, rushing to Karetnikov.

"Oo-oo-oo-oo!" he moaned like a steam engine and shook his bleeding extremity.

Larisa Yevgenevna turned to Yefim. "Fima! *You* did this?"

Fima, they said later, seemed perfectly calm. He took the bottle of vodka from the shelf, drank the rest of it, picked up his attaché case, and walked out.

That bite, I believe, did Yefim fresh—and this time irreparable—psychological damage. He came straight from Karetnikov's to my place, gleeful.

"Do you know what happened? You haven't heard?"

And he described the whole incident for me: his arrival there, the state in which he had found Karetnikov, the way Karetnikov had held his own head by the ears and banged it against the door frame. And, I have to admit it, I laughed at the head-banging part, I almost fell off my chair.

Yefim smiled and seemed very pleased with himself. Standing before me in his wide-open sheepskin, he stretched out his arms and said with a wink: "I have good porcelain teeth, comrades. Arkasha Glotov charged me four hundred rubles for them. But worth every ruble, don't you think?"

I looked at him with curiosity. Who would have thought it? He had always been so timid, yet here he was strutting, and clicking his teeth! Such a change in a man could be caused only by the stress of an emergency, I thought. This bravado was temporary, it would end soon in hysterics. Unless . . . it was the emergence of a character trait that until now had lain dormant. . . . It was also true that Yefim personally faced danger with his fearless people. He had tumbled off a cliff, had almost drowned in a polynya, had been burned at an oil well.

"Yefim," I said to him, "you're a grown man. I don't mean to lecture you. But Karetnikov is quite powerful. If you don't patch this up with him right away—"

"Not for the world!" Yefim shouted.

"He can be vindictive. He'll never forgive you!"

"I don't need anyone's forgiveness. I'm tired of being humiliated, tired of being a second-rate citizen. I have other plans."

"Other plans?"

"Yes . . ." Suspiciously he inspected all four walls and looked up at the chandelier. "Do you think your apartment's bugged?"

"How should I know?"

He told me to take the telephone to the next room, or dial a couple of numbers and then wedge a pencil in the wheel. But I didn't put much stock in such tricks—and anyway didn't really believe my phone was bugged.

"Here's an idea," I said. "It's a nice day. Why don't we take a walk?"

We went downstairs. Holding his attaché case between his legs, Yefim pulled on his leather gloves and turned up his collar. Bordered by the collar's brown fleece, his yellow pate looked like a pumpkin peeping out of a housewife's shopping bag. We walked through the courtyards to Sytinsky Lane, and from there proceeded to Tverskoy Boulevard.

The day was pleasant and sunny. The night's snowfall shone like foam on the bushes and flower beds. There were pigeons on the cleared path, schoolboys running, a young father pulling a sled at an easy trot, his child bundled up to the eyes. All the benches were occupied by chess players, old ladies, and out-of-town visitors with sacks and string shopping bags.

We walked slowly in the direction of Nikitsky Gate. At first we chatted, I don't remember what about, but then Yefim glanced around. He let two officers with briefcases walk past us, then lowered his voice and asked if I had any foreign acquaintances through whom he might send a manuscript to the West.

I did, actually, but I liked to keep such connections secret, having been using them myself to send things "over the hill," as we called it, where they were published under a pseudonym. No one knew this except my wife. Without answering yes or no, I asked Yefim what manuscript exactly he had in mind. He had nothing ready yet, he said, but needed to know in advance through whom and how to send it. Should he send the manuscript itself, or a copy on microfilm?

"A copy is better," I replied. "And one page per frame, otherwise the people who retype it will have trouble. But what are you thinking of sending?"

"I'm writing a novel, *Operation!*" He looked at me, saw the expression on my face. "You're thinking that I'm writing about decent people and no one will want it. But this isn't about decent people, it's about rotten ones."

And he told me the story, the real story, on which he had based his plot. It was quite different. The doctor performed an operation on himself, all right, but he performed it not in the middle of the ocean but off the coast of Canada. The stricken man could have been taken to a hospital on shore. But, in the first place, that would have cost the ship a lot of money, and in foreign currency. In the second place, the doctor had recently been showing signs of ideological unreliability. Avtorkhanov's book *The Technology of Power* had been found under his pillow. They were afraid that, given the chance, the doctor would defect. So Captain Kolotuntsev (Kolomiytsev's prototype) proceeded not to the coast of Canada but to the Kuril Islands. En route to the islands the doctor, desperate, operated on himself, but listened to no romantic song afterward, because he died.

"So what do you think?" Yefim asked. "Will they like that kind of story in the West? The title's dull, but I can think up something better. For example, *Hara-kiri!* Not bad, eh? And I can put in sex, too, if necessary. We had a woman cook on board, and she slept with everyone."

"A man would be better," I said. "In the West they prefer homosexual stuff."

"Good point," Yefim said gravely, stopped, took a large pad from his attaché case, and, holding his glove in his teeth, made a note of that. "Actually, we did have one homosexual. But it wasn't the cook, it was the navigator. You won't believe this, but he slept with the first mate."

"And what would you call the first mate?"

"Boris," he said, not understanding.

"I mean, you had two homosexuals, not one," I said.

"What makes you say that?" he asked, staring at me.

"You tell me the navigator was homosexual and that he slept with the first mate. So what does that make the first mate?"

"Son of a gun!" Yefim exclaimed. "Of *course!* So obvious, and I didn't even think of it. I guess it's because I was caught up in all the other details. Wait." He reached into his attaché case for the pad again.

I wasn't that surprised. Yefim's plot, from the logical point of view, had always been weak. His books were full of absurdities that could pass only in our country. And I told him this quite frankly.

I went on to say: "And even if you write such a novel, when do you expect—"

"I write fast. You know that," he said.

We had reached the end of the boulevard. Before turning back, we paused near a newsstand that carried the provincial newspapers. A man in a long coat and dark felt boots with galoshes over them was staring fixedly at the Voronezh *Pravda*. With his teeth he ripped great hunks from a loaf of bread and swallowed them. In his other hand he held a string shopping bag with more loaves.

"Let's suppose you write it fast, and it gets published over there. We still don't know if it'll be a success or not; meanwhile back here you'd lose everything. Unless you ran to Israel—"

"Under no circumstances!" Yefim said. He drew himself up. "I have shed blood for this country. I will stay here, I will struggle, and use my teeth if I have to, to uphold my human dignity. Ah, their arrogance—they won't even give me a fur hat. You've written how many books? Two? Three? And you have a fur hat. I wrote eleven, and look!" He slapped his bald head so hard, the man by the newsstand started, turned around, and began to study us, a hunk of bread dangling from his mouth.

"I don't mean *you,* sir," Yefim apologized, embarrassed.

On the way back, I let Yefim know that I had written not two books, not three, but six—which was not bad for a literary scholar. And no one had given me my goatskin hat. I bought it myself the year before last, at a bazaar in Kutaisi.

"You had an even better hat," I said. "But you gave it to Tishka."

Yefim stopped. "What, are you telling me to take back that hat?" Twirling his attaché case, he gave me a strange look.

I advised him not to do anything rash, to consider the consequences.

Lifting the sleeve of his sheepskin, he consulted his watch. "Excuse me, I have to go."

Indifferently he offered me his gloved hand, pulled

his head still deeper into his collar, and walked rapidly toward Pushkin Square.

I returned home greatly worried and called Kostya Baranov.

"Your friend," I said, "is out of his mind, in my opinion."

"Yes," Baranov agreed. "I told you. It's depression."

It wasn't depression Yefim was experiencing, I said, but the opposite, euphoria, and I feared the worst.

"What happened?"

Apparently Baranov hadn't heard yet. I couldn't relay over the telephone, of course, my conversation with Yefim on Tverskoy Boulevard. But I told Baranov about the biting of the finger.

He was very impressed. "Yefim bit Karetnikov? I don't believe it."

He hung up to call Yefim, then called me back.

"You're right, he's out of his mind. But I congratulated him anyway."

"Congratulated him!"

"Biting Karetnikov is the most inspired thing he's done in his entire literary career."

No sooner did I hang up than the phone rang again. This time it was Yefim.

"Events march!" he announced in triumph.

How exactly were they marching, I asked.

Yefim heard that Karetnikov, immediately following the bite, had phoned a certain Politburo member with whom he had been friendly ever since the war. The friend, listening, reportedly said: "Don't worry, Vasily Stepanovich, we won't leave it at that. We must not allow foreign elements to maim the sons of Russia."

"Foreign elements!" Yefim shouted. "In other words, Jews! If a Russian bites Karetnikov, that's all right, but a Jew better keep his teeth to himself."

I cautioned Yefim that this report might not be true. A member of the Politburo would hardly make such a statement, at least not on the phone. And we shouldn't discuss it on the phone either.

"I don't care," Yefim snapped. "I say what I think. I have nothing to hide."

This annoyed me. He had always been so careful, with his code words and hints, that you couldn't understand him half the time. But now, you see, he had nothing to hide. If others maybe had something to hide, that was not *his* concern.

The report of the Politburo member's statement regarding foreign elements spread rapidly throughout Moscow, and people's behavior toward Yefim changed dramatically. Some of his acquaintances stopped greeting him and shunned him like the plague. Others drew him off to a corner to congratulate him and praise his courage. Yefim changed, too. In the company of various people he began holding forth on the importance of human dignity. He remarked that civil fearlessness was far more rare these days than physical fearlessness. He spoke of men who were obedient and timid in ordinary life but in extreme circumstances became great heroes.

Meanwhile, a secret but well-coordinated rejection machine went into operation. First, the Young Guard

Publishing House told Yefim that his book would not come out this year because of a paper shortage. The LenFilm studio, which had invited him to come and discuss a film script, telephoned to let him know that the meeting was indefinitely postponed. On the radio station that was supposed to do readings from *Avalanche!,* the program was bumped in favor of a panel discussion on the evils of alcoholism. When even *Geology and Mineralogy* returned a manuscript, and one he had written on commission, Yefim knew things were serious.

Yet he became more militant than ever. He counterattacked. One night he sat down to write a letter to the Central Committee on the subject of corruption, nepotism, and toadyism in the Writers' Union. These abuses were reflected in the size of book printings, in press reviews, in the distribution of dachas, foreign assignments, and passes to the writers' lodges, and most obviously in the distribution of fur hats. The letter, however, became long-winded and tedious, so Yefim decided to write, instead, a satirical piece that he would send to *Pravda*. He inserted a sheet of paper in the typewriter and typed the title: "If the Hat Fits."

He began in a Gogolian vein:

> Do you know, gentlemen, what is meant by "if the hat fits"? We are not talking of hat size. No, they do not assign Ivan a hat in accordance with the dimensions of his cranium. How then—you may ask, dear reader—do they assign it? In accordance with Ivan's rank. To receive a respectable hat, our Ivan must be a secretary of the Writers' Union. An official, at least. His chances improve considerably if he laughs at his

superiors' jokes and belongs to the Party. But if he is not a Party member, and if—oh horror!—he happens to be a Jew . . .

Yefim paused. The part about being a Jew was not very subtle. A little delicacy was in order. It might be better to say that he had a certain insufficiency with respect to origin in his résumé. . . .

The phone rang. It was Kostya.

"Greetings, old man," Kostya said. "There's turbulence in the air."

"Turbulence?" Yefim did not understand.

"Choppiness. Very noticeable."

Yefim slammed down the receiver, turned on the radio, twisted the knob in search of German Wave. He found it, but the Wave was concluding a broadcast with a brief news summary in which there was nothing of particular interest. The BBC was having a jazz concert. On the Voice of America's band there was the unbroken howl of jamming. Yefim picked up the radio and began running around the room with it, turning it this way, that way, now holding it against the radiator, now swiveling the antenna down. He even banged the set against his knee; sometimes that helped. Nothing worked. But it was only a quarter to nine, not the best time. Yefim turned the radio off, and at nine turned it back on. This time the Voice of America came through almost without static. Yefim listened to a report on the new American proposal for the reduction of intermediate-range missiles . . . tension in the Persian Gulf . . . increased activity of Afghan rebels . . . flooding in the Philippines. Then:

"From Moscow. Leading Soviet writer Yefim Rakhlin, according to reliable sources, has committed a physical assault on the person of the secretary of the Writers' Union, Vasily Karelin. Observers believe that the attack was motivated by frustration over the lack of artistic freedom of writers in the Soviet Union."

"Kukusha!" Yefim shouted. "Kukusha!"

"What happened?" cried Kukusha as she ran in, alarmed.

"They! They!" Yefim stammered, pointing to the radio. "Just now—they said—about me!"

"Said what?" Kukusha asked blankly.

"They called me 'leading Soviet writer Yefim Rakhlin.' And they mentioned Karetnikov, too, got his name wrong. Can you imagine? Leading Soviet writer Yefim Rakhlin!"

Kukusha looked at her husband coldly.

"Baldy," she said finally, "if they send you to Mordovia, I'm not following you there."

Mordovia? Yefim had not prepared himself for that eventuality. Still, if they sent him to Mordovia, he would have liked to know that Kukusha would stand by him. . . .

Then Tishka walked in, the wolf-fur hat in his hands. "Papa! If you don't stop, I'll have to denounce you. Either that, or ask Natasha for an invitation to Israel." And he put the hat on a chair and left.

Yefim let himself down on the couch and sat for a long time, hands at his temples.

"All right," he said quietly, with a bitter smile. "My son denounces me. My wife won't follow me. No, she prefers the capital, where she keeps company with generals. . . . Slut!" he roared. Jumping up, he clenched his fists, stamped his feet. "Out, out of my study!"

"Fima!" Kukusha cried. "You have no right to talk to me like that!"

"And you," Yefim shouted, "have no right to be in here! Here, where my beautiful heroes live!"

An evening full of fireworks.

When he calmed down, Yefim ran to the bedroom, where Kukusha lay sobbing. He tugged at her, begged her forgiveness. She pushed him away, shouting hysterically. Tishka locked himself in his room and turned on the Beatles full blast so he wouldn't have to listen to this. Kukusha went on sobbing, so Yefim returned to the radio in his study. Now all the stations were talking about the writer Rakhlin, but much of what they said was untrue—for example, that he was being persecuted for his adherence to Judaism, or that he was a friend of Academician Andrei Sakharov. Yefim had never laid eyes on the famous physicist.

The phone rang nonstop. Kostya called four times. Other well-wishers called, people he knew and people he didn't. American news correspondents from the Associated Press, Germans from the ADN. A man's voice said: "You don't know me, but I want to say that all honest people are with you." Another voice, cheerful: "Keep this up, Yid, and we'll circumcise your head!"

Kukusha came running in and knelt before Yefim. "I entreat you. For the sake of your children, repent. Go to Karetnikov. Ask his forgiveness. Tell him you didn't know what you were doing."

"Never!" Yefim said, and drove her out again. Then

ran to apologize again. Then answered the phone again. Then listened to the radio again.

He spent the night in his study, on the couch. Not taking off his clothes, he covered himself with a woolen lap robe, the radio beside him, and kept turning the knob from band to band. He even picked up Radio Liberty, which he usually couldn't get. In an English-language broadcast he understood only one sentence, but what an important sentence it was for him: "Mr. Rakh*leen* is a fearless man."

Yefim lay awake for a long time, scratching himself and thinking about the fame that had descended on him so unexpectedly. He was in trouble, no question. But the whole world knew him now.

He woke up late. Kukusha and Tishka were already gone. While he fried his eggs and brewed his coffee, he received several phone calls. Then a telegram was delivered, which read: STEADY AS YOU GO EXCL MITYA. "EXCL" meant "exclamation point," but Yefim could not place Mitya. While he ate his eggs and tried to think, Fishkin came bursting in, scared out of his wits.

"Fima, what are you doing!" he hissed. "Do you realize that there are eight million people in the Party? It's an army, a mobilized army. Do you have any idea against what you are lifting your hand?"

"Solomon Yevseevich," Yefim said. "What do the eighteen million people in the Party have to do with it? I'm not opposing them. All I want from them is a good fur hat, not fluffy tomcat. Rabbit, at least, like Kostya's.

Especially since Kostya is unknown," he added with a smug grin, "and I'm a writer with a world reputation."

"You're a fool with a world reputation!" Fishkin shouted. "You think because the Voice of America talked about you, it means something? It means nothing! When *they* get hold of you, no Voice of America will be able to help you. They'll squash you like a bedbug."

"First you compare me to an ugly duckling, and now to a bedbug."

The fairy-tale writer had hardly left when again the doorbell rang. Cursing under his breath, Yefim went to the door, opened it, and recoiled. Before him, hunched and crooked, winking evilly, left cheek twitching, stood Vaska Tryoshkin. Unshaven, he wore greasy flannel pajamas of uncertain color and bedroom slippers.

"You want to see *me?*" Yefim asked in disbelief.

Vaska nodded.

"Well, come in," Yefim said, stepping aside. "You'll have to excuse me, I haven't cleaned up my study yet. This way, please, to the kitchen."

Vaska, walking down the hall, saw the starfishes mounted on the wall. To his surprise, they did not have six points but only five.

Yefim offered his neighbor a stool and cleared the frying pan from the table.

"Would you like some tea? Coffee? Or something a bit stronger?" Yefim winked.

Vaska shook his head. "No, nothing. Yesterday I heard about you from *there.*" He pointed to the ceiling. "Apparently you are known there."

"Apparently," Yefim said, not without pride.

"Who'd have thought it?" Vaska lowered his voice. "Do you have a piece of paper?"

"Writing paper?"

"And . . ." Vaska said. He moved his hand, miming the act of writing.

"And a pen?" Yefim said.

Vaska frowned and pointed with both hands at the walls and ceiling, where microphones might be located.

Yefim ran to his study, afraid that in his absence Vaska would put poison in the coffee maker. He grabbed the first sheet of paper that came to hand—not from the stack of new, untouched paper, which he prized, but from the pile that lay at the edge of the desk. These sheets contained a few trivial notes or jottings, but still had space on them to serve for household memos or even short letters.

"Here." Yefim put the paper, clean side up, in front of Vaska and also gave him a pen. Vaska cast another suspicious look around, squinted at the light bulb, which might hold a concealed lens, then waved a hand, wrote, and pushed the paper toward Yefim.

Yefim slapped his pockets, ran to get his glasses, and finally read: "Request acceptance into Yid-Masons."

He looked at Vaska. "I don't understand."

Vaska pulled the paper back, added, "Please!" He put a hand on his heart and nodded.

Yefim shrugged, hands outspread, to indicate total incomprehension.

"He doesn't trust me," Vaska thought.

The phone rang.

"Excuse me." Yefim ran to his study again.

The ring was soft, ominous.

"Hello, Yefim. This is Lukin."

"Yes?" said Yefim, on his guard.

"Yefim." In Lukin's voice, false cheer. "I think it's time we got together."

"Oh?" Yefim sneered. "Has something happened?"

"Yefim Semyonovich." Lukin was controlling his temper. "You know very well that something has happened. A great deal worth talking about has happened."

Meanwhile, Vaska Tryoshkin, sitting in the kitchen, was racking his brains about how to convince Rakhlin of his sincerity. In despair, he picked up the piece of paper, to tear it in two, but happened to glance at it first against the light—and was stunned. Traced on the back were characters of some sort, seemingly Russian, but from right to left, in the Hebrew manner. A reply to his request!

He turned the paper over and read, this time from left to right: "The first five letters, a large-scale musical work. The next six letters, a soldier's fare. Together, a nine-letter word for surgery." Vaska, adding five and six, got eleven, not nine. "Hebrew mathematics," he thought in awe. This was clearly beyond him. But he had to try to figure it out. Probably, one was accepted into the Yid-Masons only if he passed this test. As a last resort, Vaska could ask Cherpakov. He folded the paper in four, tucked it into his pajama pocket, and started for the door. He could hear the Zionist Rakhlin talking on the telephone.

Lukin was saying, "Understand me, Yefim. I'm calling for your own good. We must try to save you."

"I don't need saving," Yefim replied. "I need respect. I need a respectable hat."

"The problem, Yefim, isn't the hat, it's the head that wears the hat. I want to help you. Come see me tomorrow, and we'll discuss what to do next."

"When tomorrow?"

"Why don't we say at sixteen hundred hours?"

The thought occurred to Yefim (and he jotted it down in his notepad) that if Lukin had not been an important official, he would have said simply "at four o'clock." A telling detail.

Vaska tiptoed quietly past the open door. He waved to signal Yefim not to bother, he'd let himself out.

"All right," Yefim said into the receiver. "I'll be there."

In Lukin's office, in addition to Lukin himself, Yefim found Party Committee secretary Samarin, Secretariat members Victor Shubin and Victor Cherpakov, critics Bromberg and Solyony, Natalya Knysh, and a man Yefim did not know, whose blond hair was parted on the side and neatly slicked down.

Yefim did not immediately see Karetnikov. Karetnikov was standing by the window, in a dark foreign suit, with his Hero of Socialist Labor star, deputy's badge, and laureate medal. His right arm lay in a black silk sling; his finger, skillfully but somewhat ostentatiously bandaged, protruded like an awkward birch bough.

Yefim was disconcerted to see so many people. From his telephone conversation with Lukin he had expected a private tête-à-tête. Should he wait here for the people to leave, or go sit in the corridor? Looking at no one, Yefim made for Lukin's desk to ask. But Lukin raised a hand and said hastily, as if fearing Yefim's teeth, "No, sit over there." He pointed to a chair at a small table off to one side.

Yefim sat. No one spoke. Lukin was writing hurriedly. Karetnikov took a pack of Marlboros from his pocket with his left hand, shook them, and with his teeth extracted a cigarette. Then he produced a box of matches and, deftly gripping the box in the crook of his right arm, as if he had been disabled for years, struck a light. Solyony and Bromberg lit up, too. The blond man took out a comb and combed his hair.

A secretary entered, laid a paper in front of Lukin, and asked something in a whisper. Lukin replied loudly, "Tell them I can't possibly today. I have a personal case." Yefim looked at him in surprise. What personal case? Yefim's? But Lukin had said nothing, over the phone, about scheduling a formal hearing. Yefim looked around nervously and noticed that the people present were avoiding his eyes. Bromberg lowered his head; Natalya Knysh turned away and blushed; Shubin was busy cleaning his nails. Cherpakov alone looked straight at Yefim, brazen and cheerful, for this was an event dear to his heart: when many come together to crush one.

Cherpakov's colleagues were not so bloodthirsty. Under different circumstances they would not have chosen to be here. But Natalya Knysh, planning to take a trip abroad, needed a character reference, and those were impossible to obtain if one shirked one's duties in the collective. Solyony, who had been apprehended after many years of appropriating Party dues and speculating in icons, nourished hopes of being rehabilitated. And Bromberg had come running simply out of fear. Years ago, he had been accused of cosmopolitanism, Zionism, and petit-bourgeois nationalism. His writings had been pulled apart, misrepresented, distorted beyond recognition. (His pernicious activity had been investigated by a commission under the leadership of none other than Cherpakov.) Bromberg's attempts to vindicate himself had been taken as proofs of low cunning, hypocrisy, duplicity. He had suffered such fear that he was now willing, if only they left him in peace, to pull apart whomever they liked.

The secretary left. For a while Lukin stared at the paper she had put before him, then he looked up at Yefim and said, "How are you, Comrade Rakhlin?"

Yesterday Yefim had been Yefim, today he was Comrade Rakhlin.

Yefim shrugged, fearing a trap.

"You shrug. You have a health problem?"

"No-o." Yefim decided to be careful what he said.

"How long since you last saw a psychiatrist?" the blond man asked unexpectedly. He got out his comb again.

"And who are you?" Yefim asked.

"That is not important," the blond man said.

The door opened, and someone dressed in gray stepped in soundlessly. He nodded as if to everyone yet to no one in particular, then slipped along the wall and sat down behind Bromberg. No one got up, no one was alarmed; they all acted as though nothing had happened. Even so, there was a new tension in the room, the sense, almost, of an other-worldly presence.

The moment the man in gray entered, Karetnikov reached over to a potted ficus tree and put out his cigarette, Solyony stubbed out his cigarette against the leg of a chair, and Bromberg tiptoed over to Lukin's desk and crushed his cigarette in a marble ashtray practically under the general's nose. The general looked at Bromberg in surprise, frowned, and pushed the ashtray away. Addressing everyone, he said softly: "Comrades, we are here to examine the statement of Vasily Stepanovich Karetnikov, who is present. I will now read it to you."

Karetnikov left the window and quietly sat behind the man in gray. As Lukin, removing his glasses and squinting, read aloud, Yefim took a pen and pad from his attaché case and began to take notes.

Karetnikov's statement was written in a stilted, bureaucratic manner with pretensions to style. A so-called man of letters, it said, one Rakhlin, taking advantage of Karetnikov's trusting nature and the unflagging generosity which he, Karetnikov, always showed to writers of the younger generation, had entered his, Karetnikov's, apartment under the pretext of acquainting him with his, that is, Rakhlin's, new manuscript. Rakhlin, however, did not produce said manuscript, but instead demanded that the abused victim, Karetnikov, use his influence to obtain for him, Rakhlin, certain undeserved privileges. Upon receiving a firm refusal, the perpetrator switched from demands to threats and from threats to abusive actions, finally committing an entirely unprovoked assault upon the person of the abused, a most outrageous, humiliating assault, which required said victim to seek the ministrations of a physician, not to mention loss of his capacity to perform his regular literary, administrative, and community duties. "I appeal to my comrades and colleagues," Karetnikov's statement concluded, "to examine Rakhlin's behavior and to pass judgment on that behavior, and it is my hope it will be a judgment that will defend the honor and dignity of an active member of our united and high-minded writers' organization."

All this was heard in funereal silence.

"Vasily Stepanovich," Lukin asked, "have you anything to add to your statement?"

"My finger," Karetnikov said, "is swollen and infected, and I had to have a shot of antibiotic."

"In a case like this, you should play it safe and have a rabies shot, too," Bromberg quipped. But no one laughed, because although the joke was directed at Yefim, it clearly hit Karetnikov as well, and the overall effect was unfortunate.

Karetnikov continued: "With this bandage, I can't write. And tomorrow I have a district Party conference and an appointment with the Afro-Asian writers' delegation. Then the Secretariat, a conference of the Lenin Prize committee, and a session of the Supreme Soviet. How can I sit in the Supreme Soviet looking like this? My wife told me to phone the prosecutor general immediately. That's probably what I should have done. But, frankly, I didn't want to wash our dirty linen in public. The reputation of our union is dear to my heart. The Secretariat, I hope, will be able to see that justice is done without recourse to the intervention of the legal authorities." Vasily Stepanovich cast a look of supplication at the back of the head of the man in gray before him, then resumed his seat.

"And we will," Lukin said. He too looked at the man in gray. "But before proceeding with our investigation, I should add to Vasily Stepanovich's statement the fact that this scandalous incident has become the property of hostile Western propaganda. Some of you heard yesterday, I think, a certain anti-Soviet foreign radio station—"

"Personally, I never listen to such broadcasts," Natalya Knysh felt it necessary to remark.

"No decent person listens to that garbage," Solyony added darkly.

Lukin looked at Yefim. "And you, Comrade Rakhlin, did you not hear something of the sort?"

"Excuse me?" Yefim lifted his pen from the paper and looked at Lukin.

"Did you not hear," Lukin repeated in a rasping voice, "something of the sort?"

"Was that your question? Just a second, I'll write it down. . . . 'Did you not hear something of the sort?' " He raised his eyes to Lukin. "Of what sort?"

Flustered, Lukin looked at the man in gray, then back at Yefim. "You are being asked—" he began.

"Just a second. 'You are being asked . . .' " Yefim entered this painstakingly on his pad.

". . . being asked whether indeed you did not also . . . Put that pad away!" Lukin said, losing his temper. "We didn't invite you here to practice dictation!"

". . . didn't invite you here to practice dictation," Yefim repeated as he wrote.

"Comrades, this is hooliganism!" Bromberg shouted. "Confiscate that notepad! Or make him put it away!"

"No," Cherpakov said ironically. "Let him keep it, let him write. The Pentagon, the CIA, and the Voice of America need an exact account."

Yefim's hand began to tremble, but he continued to move the pen across the paper. He could not keep up, though, because everyone now talked at once. Knysh accused him of disrespect to the group. Shubin said that Yefim had been to Poland and probably participated in the criminal activities of Solidarity. Yefim, writing furiously, missed the reference to Solidarity. Then Solyony stood up.

"Comrades," he said. "Our agenda says we are here to censure Rakhlin's act of hooliganism. But what he has done is more than an act of hooliganism. Consider. Vasily Stepanovich Karetnikov is a foremost writer. His impassioned, ardent books have instilled in millions of Soviet citizens love of the fatherland. Rakhlin bit the hand that created these works. Why? Because he wasn't given a hat?"

"Nonsense!" Bromberg sputtered.

"Especially since *I* am not in charge of any hats," Karetnikov said with a pitying smile.

"It's perfectly clear," Solyony went on, "that Rakhlin acted not on his own behalf but as an agent of enemies of our literature, enemies of our system."

"Yes!" Cherpakov agreed. "This isn't hooliganism, it's terrorism! Political terrorism! People were shot for such things in our country, in the good old days."

At this, Yefim stopped writing. He put the pad on

the empty chair beside him and looked first at Cherpakov, then at Lukin, then at Karetnikov. The man in gray had disappeared. In his place the blond man sat and combed his hair.

Yefim had prepared himself for unpleasantness, but not for accusations like these. Suddenly he was frightened. He started to quake, to babble uncontrollably. His comrades had misunderstood him, he said. He was no agent of enemy powers, but had acted on his own, and he admitted that what he had done was outrageous, but he pleaded temporary insanity, because having been a member of the Writers' Union for eighteen years and written eleven books, eleven books, mind you, about decent Soviet people, people of fearless professions, he—

"Why do you tell us all this?" Lukin growled.

"He's covering his tracks!" Cherpakov laughed. "Zigging and zagging, Zionist tactics!"

"Silence!" Yefim shouted, and stamped his foot.

"And why should I be silent?" Cherpakov said, stepping forward. "I didn't come here to be silent."

"Silence!" Yefim shouted again. His whole body stiffened. He put his hands out before him. And with another "Silence!" he rushed at Cherpakov.

And now the most extraordinary thing happened.

Cherpakov turned pale, shrieked, "He's gonna bite me!" and dove under Lukin's desk. Lukin was dumbfounded. "Victor Petrovich, Victor Petrovich, get hold of yourself!" he shouted, and kicked at Cherpakov. But Yefim too dove under the desk. The hunter's instinct had taken command of him, and he really was set on biting Cherpakov. But as he dove, something happened. A sweet taste filled his mouth. Then there was a flash of light, like arc welding. A second, a third . . . until the flashes merged into one majestic radiance and Yefim's body became weightless. Transformed into a white swan, he came out from under the desk and rose into the air. The committee members receded into the distance, craning their necks and staring at Yefim with open mouths.

Yefim was taken to the intensive-care unit at Botkin Hospital. The diagnosis: a stroke, with loss of speech and partial paralysis of the left arm.

"The situation," Kukusha was told by a young physician with a red smoke-stained mustache who reeked of tobacco, "is grave." And after a moment's thought he added, "Extremely."

"What can I do for him?" Kukusha asked, wringing her hands.

"You?" He smiled. "You cannot upset him."

"Yes, I understand. What he needs is complete rest and positive thoughts."

"Rest, yes," the doctor said, lighting a cheap cigarette. "As for thoughts . . . He'd be better off without thoughts right now. Positive or negative."

Kukusha, however, did not agree with the doctor. She had boundless faith in the curative power of positive thoughts.

When she and Tishka were allowed in to see the patient, she hardly recognized him. Yefim was all tangled in tubes and wires, and his head was so bandaged he looked like a man from outer space.

The wife and son, both wearing threadbare hospital gowns over their clothes, sat by the patient's bed. He stared indifferently at the ceiling.

"The doctor says it's not serious," Kukusha told Yefim. "Everything will be all right. The main thing is for you not to worry. At home, all is well. Incidentally, Young Guard called yesterday and said your manuscript has gone to the printer. And a letter arrived from the manager of LenFilm, your script has been given to the director. And what else? Oh, yes, I got the clothes from the laundry. Tishka's doing well, too. Aren't you, Tishka?"

"Yes," Tishka said.

"Tell your father about your paper," she said.

"It's nothing special," Tishka said. "They're publishing it in the proceedings."

"He's being modest," Kukusha said. "Academician Trunov said Tishka's paper was worth more than some thick doctoral dissertations. He said that, didn't he, Tishka?"

Tishka nodded. "Yes."

"So everything's fine with us. You don't need to worry. Lie still and get well. As soon as you can eat, I'll bring you something good. Would you like bouillon? Or maybe something sweet? Or better still, something on the tart side? Should I make you some cranberry punch? Yes or no? Can't you talk a little, to let me know what you want?"

Yefim frowned, mumbled something.

"What?" Kukusha asked, bending down to him.

"H—ha."

"What?" Kukusha looked at Tishka. Tishka shrugged.

"What did you say? Come on, make an effort, try to say it more clearly."

"Hha," Yefim said.

"Oh, hat!" Kukusha guessed, and rejoiced. "You still want your hat! So you do have desires! Wonderful! You'll get well, you'll recover, and you'll have your hat. No, no, I won't go and buy one, I'll make *them* bring it to you. Lukin will bring it personally, I promise."

An elderly nurse entered the room with a collection of syringes.

"That's all now," she said softly. "Visiting hours are over. Yefim and I have our little procedures to do."

I heard that Kukusha went straight from the hospital to Lukin, who received her with great reluctance. She scolded the general and demanded that the Secretariat issue a fur hat to her poor husband as restitution. "He's critically ill," she said. "He needs positive thoughts."

The general put on a face of stone, indicating that no displays of misguided humanism could be expected of him. "I am sorry, but I can do nothing. We tried to help him, but he persisted in his defiance and wouldn't confess his guilt."

"Guilt? What guilt?!" Kukusha exclaimed. "So he bit Karetnikov because of a hat. But now he's dying, *dying*, and surely you don't think my husband deserves the *death* penalty?"

Lukin did not reply to this. He stared past Kukusha, and from his face she could tell that he did not care whether or not Yefim died.

"Listen, Pyotr Nikolaevich!" Kukusha abandoned her chair and went right up to Lukin's desk. "What kind of man are you? Why are you so cruel? You too, in your time, suffered."

It seemed to Kukusha that these words got through to him.

"Yes," he said, and assumed a dignified air. "I suffered. But I suffered for principles, not for a hat. And when I suffered, I never . . ." His lower lip started trembling. "I never once doubted our high ideals. Look. My daughter." He pulled out his wallet.

"His daughter!" Kukusha mimicked, flying into a fury. "A little girl in a little bow! But killing a man—that's easy for you, you son of a bitch!" She reached across the desk and seized him by the lapels. "If you don't personally bring my husband a hat, so help me I'll—"

The general struggled to free himself. "Zinaida Ivanovna! What are you doing! How dare you!"

Kukusha came to her senses. She spat at Lukin and rushed from the office in tears. In Insurrection Square, she grabbed a taxi, collapsed into the backseat, and cried all the way home. She had no idea what to do. She couldn't buy a hat with her own money and say that the Writers' Union had issued it to her. Yefim would know.

The taxi drove into the courtyard and pulled up behind a black Volga. Kukusha paid and started toward the entrance, but the door of the Volga opened and a tall man in a dark coat and narrow-brimmed hat blocked her way.

"Zinaida Ivanovna, I am Colonel Kolesnichenko."

Kukusha took a step back. "A KGB colonel?"

The man smiled. "No, infantry. Aide to Marshal Pobratimov. He has arrived and is waiting for you at the Hotel Moscow."

This was not the best time for a rendezvous, but Kukusha went into action. "All right, I'll be down in a few minutes."

"Very good, ma'am."

She dashed upstairs, threw off her clothes, and was back in no time, giving off the mingled scent of soap and perfume.

The marshal occupied a deluxe three-room suite. In the vestibule, on a four-pronged polished rack, hung two greatcoats and two tall sheepskin hats. The owners of the hats were sitting in a sumptuous living room at an oval table covered with hors d'oeuvres enough for twelve. They were drinking French cognac in tumblers. One bottle had already been emptied and another begun. The room was dense with smoke; wavy blue-gray layers of smoke floated beneath and around a many-tiered crystal chandelier.

"Zina, my love!"

One of the revelers, a large man with a shaven head who looked like Yul Brynner, rose to greet Kukusha. Pobratimov wore a green uniform shirt with marshal's epaulets but no necktie. His parade jacket, heavy with medals, hung on the back of a chair near the Becker piano.

Unabashed by the presence of his drinking companion and Kolesnichenko, the marshal embraced Kukusha and kissed her full on the lips.

"Phew!" She couldn't help pulling back.

"You must have brandy breath, Comrade Marshal," the companion said, approaching Kukusha. This was Pobratimov's former aide, Ivan Fedoseevich, now a major general. "Good day, Zina, my dear." He raised Kukusha's hand to his mouth and kissed it wetly.

"Yes, the fumes must be pretty strong. I didn't even think," the marshal said, embarrassed. He was drunk but in complete possession of himself. "Now here's a splash of cognac for you, my love. Let's be fragrant together."

He poured a half-tumbler for Kukusha, for Ivan Fedoseevich, and for himself. Then he looked at Kolesnichenko, who was still standing at the door.

"Comrade Marshal, I still have to visit my sister," Kolesnichenko said. "Permission to disappear?"

"Granted," the marshal said.

Kolesnichenko disappeared.

The marshal raised his glass. "Well, Zina, my love, to our reunion! But why are you so down in the mouth?"

Kukusha drained the whole half-tumbler in one gulp, then turned to Pobratimov. "I've got trouble, Marshal. My husband—" her lip quivered "—just had a stroke." She burst into a howl.

Another half-tumbler was poured for her, and she was asked to tell the whole story. The men listened attentively.

"You mean he brought himself to this on account of a hat?" the marshal asked in surprise.

"It happens," Ivan Fedoseevich remarked. "I remember we had a lieutenant colonel who was expecting a hat, too—a colonel's *papakha*. When they didn't give him one, he put a bullet through his head."

"A fool," Pobratimov said.

"Obviously, a fool," Ivan Fedoseevich agreed. "Especially since there'd been a mistake. They'd given him the promotion, but forgotten to include him on the list. So he received his *papakha* posthumously, you might say. It was put on the lid of his coffin."

"A fool, anyway," the marshal said, shaking his head. "Better a live lieutenant colonel than a dead colonel."

After the third bottle was opened, Kukusha's story about Lukin's heartlessness was heard.

"And who is Lukin?" the marshal asked sternly.

"That KGB general, maybe?" Ivan Fedoseevich wondered.

"You know him?"

"Yes, Comrade Marshal. If he's the one, I know him very well indeed. He came to me once, asked me to exempt his grandson from the draft. The boy's a photographer, athlete, mountain climber, and Komsomol leader."

"I see," the marshal said. "And you exempted him?"

"Yes, Comrade Marshal, I did. But that error can be rectified."

The marshal said to Kukusha, nodding in Ivan Fedoseevich's direction: "Shrewd fellow! What an aide I lost! Excellent, Ivan, send the little bastard a draft notice, would you? And when Grandpa comes running, tell him we'll ship the kid to Afghanistan. And if he doesn't personally take the hat to the hospital, tell him that Marshal Pobratimov will eat him for breakfast."

"Yes, Comrade Marshal! Yes, sir!" Ivan Fedoseevich said happily. "I won't use quite those words, but I'll get the point across. What kind of hat do you want, dear?" he asked playfully, turning to Kukusha. "Fin, feather, or fawn?"

As a result of the above conversation, a letter was delivered by messenger and signed for by a young cameraman and graduate student named Petya. Following the instructions in this letter, Petya presented himself at the Military Registration and Enlistment Office and was received personally, to his surprise, by none other than the military commissar of the city of Moscow, Major General Danilov.

The general was extremely cordial. He came out from behind his desk, shook Petya's hand, seated him on the couch, and sat down right beside him.

"So you're a cameraman?" the general asked, turning the light of his gold smile up on Petya. "A splendid profession. Not as safe, though, as some people think. I remember we had a cameraman at the front. A man of exceptional courage. Sometimes, to get a good close-up, he would practically lie down under an enemy tank or expose himself to the machine guns. A remarkable man." The general sighed. "He perished, unfortunately."

Continuing with his questions, the general learned that the young cameraman possessed many other skills: Petya was a mountain climber, knew karate, had been active in community work, and was on the executive board of the Moscow Komsomol.

"Why, you seem *destined* for us!" The general clasped his hands together in a thoroughly unmilitary manner. "We want to record the difficult work of our soldiers fighting abroad, so we need a good cameraman. Someone, too, to show the struggle in the mountains. Your experience as a mountain climber will be invaluable. And finally, we need people who have been hardened ideologically, who are devoted to our principles and ready to lay down their lives for them."

"You're sending me to Afghanistan?" Petya asked in a weak voice.

For the first time, the smile faded from the general's face. "Young man," he said quietly, "in the army one does not ask the obvious."

All things in life are connected. If Kukusha hadn't seen Marshal Pobratimov and Ivan Fedoseevich, Lukin's grandson wouldn't have been summoned to the military commissariat. If the grandson hadn't been summoned, the grandfather would have had no reason to go there, too. And if Lukin hadn't gone there, he would have had no reason to then phone Andrey Andreevich Shchupov. The result of all these encounters and phone calls was the rush order and manufacture, by the co-op of the USSR LitFund, of one special-order reindeer-fawn hat, size seven and a half.

When it came my turn to visit Yefim, he had already received his hat. Pyotr Nikolaevich Lukin had personally delivered it to him in his room, had sat beside him and told him stories about his military past. Through this noble act Pyotr Nikolaevich consolidated his authority among the writers. Despite everything, though he was KGB, he wasn't a bad sort, unlike some. Yes, if ordered to shoot, he would shoot. But on his own initiative, Pyotr Nikolaevich wouldn't hurt a fly. And if there was the chance to do some good, he'd do it.

———

Yefim lay in a small room which he shared with a convalescing old man, who left when I appeared. Yefim's head was bandaged so much that only his eyes, mouth, and nose were left uncovered. A plastic tube had been inserted in his nose and fastened with tape. Another tube, from a bottle suspended above him, was taped to his left wrist. His right arm, I saw, was not paralyzed: with it he was stroking the reindeer-fawn hat, which lay on his chest.

Not knowing how to entertain him, I began by talking about the chess tournament, which had been won by his favorite grand master, Spassky. Seeing him take no interest in the tournament, I switched to a story about the manager of our apartment house, who was renting out his office to prostitutes for a percentage of their take.

Yefim listened politely, but in his eyes I saw reproach. I became ill at ease, feeling that with that look he was asking: Why tell me such trivial nonsense, when here I am about to leave this world for another?

I was ashamed, but somehow couldn't bring myself to speak seriously. I told him an utterly stupid anecdote about Margaret Thatcher and Neil Kinnock, inventing it right on the spot. Finally, seeing that my exertions were producing no response in the patient other than the desire to be delivered from them, I decided it was time to leave.

"Well, old man," I said in an insufferably false tone, "enough of this. Next time, we'll meet at home. We'll smoke a cigarette and have a game of chess."

I touched his shoulder and made for the door. I was turning the knob when behind me I heard a shrill, agonized sound. Looking back in alarm, I saw Yefim gesturing, beckoning with the finger of his good right hand.

"Umm!" he moaned, and poked at the hat with his finger.

"You'd like me to put it on the night table?" I asked.

"Umm!" He swung his hand in the negative.

As I stared, uncomprehending, he poked at the hat again and showed me two limply spread fingers.

"You mean that you have two hats now?"

His reply this time was not a moan but an angry howl, and he flapped his hand in frustration at my obtuseness. Obviously he needed to convey some important thought.

"Umm! Umm! Umm!" It was a cry wrenched from the heart. Two half-bent fingers, like two commas, waved before my eyes.

"Ah!" I said, not trusting my own guess. "You mean—you won!"

"Umm!" he growled in a satisfied way, and dropped his hand on the hat.

As I left, I glanced back once more. Eyes closed, hat clasped to his chest, Yefim lay quiet and calm. He was smiling.

That very night he died.

Yefim was given a modest funeral—he did not lie in state at the Central Literary Club, nor did a band play for him. It was already the end of March. A wan sun was shining, and slow rivulets trickled from under the dark snow that banked against the walls of the morgue. The gates of the morgue were wide open; the funeral bus was late.

Among the people gathered around the coffin I saw Baranov, Fishkin, Mylnikov. I don't remember who else. At the head of the coffin stood Kukusha, in a black hat with a black veil that fell over her eyes, and Tishka, who held in the hand tucked behind his back (I noticed) not the reindeer-fawn hat but the wolf-fur hat his father had given him. Yefim's face, no longer bandaged, seemed appeased.

I placed my little bouquet at the feet of the deceased, embraced Kukusha, and shook Tishka's hand. As I greeted the others, I saw Vaska Tryoshkin too. He had arrived after me, apparently, and his behavior was stranger than usual. Hunched and crooked, he was twitching and looking around as though he planned to steal something or else had stolen it already. When he approached the coffin, he bent over the deceased and kissed his brow. Then gazed long and searchingly at those stiffened features, as if trying to read something in them.

Someone touched my elbow. It was Kukusha.

"Don't you think he's acting peculiar?" she whispered, indicating Vaska with her eyes.

"He's always acting peculiar," I said.

Vaska hurriedly made the sign of the cross over Yefim—not with the usual three fingers but with his whole hand. Then he thrust his hand into the coffin, somewhere under the deceased's neck, and immediately pulled it out again.

"Did you see that?" Kukusha whispered. "He put something in there."

"We'll find out right now."

I went up to the coffin and looked at Vaska, who was watching me nervously. As he watched, I reached in, felt under Yefim's neck, and pulled out a sheet of paper folded several times.

"Stop! Stop!" Vaska came running over. "Don't touch it! It's not yours."

"What is it?" I hid the paper behind my back.

"None of your business," Vaska growled. "Give it to me, it's mine."

"You have no right," Kukusha said, coming over, "putting your hand in other people's coffins without permission, not to mention inserting unauthorized objects."

She took the paper from me and unfolded it. I peered over her shoulder and saw a word written in large slanting letters, with an exclamation point at the end: "Operation!"

Vaska twitched with embarrassment.

"What does this mean?" Kukusha said, frowning.

"It's a riddle that he gave me. And I solved it, but he died. So I thought, well, why not put it in anyway, maybe he'll read it on the other side. Maybe he'll give me a sign. Let me have it!" he pleaded. "Let me put it back in! It won't do any harm!"

Outside the gate we heard the rumbling of the bus, which had just arrived.

"It will be burned anyway," Kukusha sighed. Returning the paper to Vaska, she started toward the exit.

While the bus turned around and backed up, a black Volga drove into the courtyard and stopped. Pyotr Nikolaevich Lukin climbed out of the Volga, removing a crushed blue beret from his head. He approached, looked at the deceased, and conferred in whispers with Kukusha. Then he stood at the head of the coffin and gave a speech, in which he enumerated all Yefim's merits, not forgetting his wartime service, his eighteen years in the Writers' Union, and his eleven published books. Pyotr Nikolaevich also said that the deceased had been a fearless, decent man. That, being good, he had seen only the good in life. I thought that Pyotr Nikolaevich would then say something about people who saw only the bad in life because they themselves were bad; and I thought that as he said this he would look in my direction. But he didn't. He concluded his speech with the promise that the memory of Yefim Semyonovich Rakhlin would remain in our hearts forever.

We rode to the crematorium in two buses. I happened to be in the one that carried the coffin.

On the Sadovaya Circle we made almost all the green lights and moved along quickly. Yefim lay in front of me with his elevated head, sharpened nose, closed eyes, and an expression as though he were pondering some serious and important idea. In the traffic, the bus alternately sped up and slowed down. Patches of sunlight streamed in. They skimmed over his peaceful face like a reflection of his thoughts. Vaska Tryoshkin, sitting across from me, stared intensely at that face. Next to him Kostya Baranov and Tishka carried on an inaudible conversation, Fishkin gazed apathetically out the window, and Mylnikov's whisper poured into my ear as he recited for me, neglecting no detail, an article about him that had been published in the *New York Review of Books*.